PAVLA MELECKA

THE BOND

iUniverse books may be ordered through booksellers or by contacting:

iUniverse
1663 Liberty Drive
Bloomington, IN 47403
www.iuniverse.com
1-800-Authors (1-800-288-4677)

ISBN: 978-1-5320-6495-1 (sc)
ISBN: 978-1-5320-6497-5 (hc)
ISBN: 978-1-5320-6496-8 (e)

Library of Congress Control Number: 2019900784

Print information available on the last page.

iUniverse rev. date: 02/06/2019

To my husband, the most generous, supportive and loving person I know, who made my dream come true.

*From the beginning of time,
men have tied their lives to horses. Horses
helped us overcome distances, did hard work for us,
fought and died with us in wars. Nowadays, they give us
the joy of riding, they are our partners in equestrian sports,
our companions. But there is much more. A bond, similar to
true love, which can develop between a rider and his horse.
It is like the horse was born to be ridden by you, and you
were born to ride that horse. Your minds are so well
connected there is no need to spur the horse on. You
just think of doing it and it will respond. Such a
horse is absolutely devoted to you. Give it your
love and it will do anything for you.*

CONTENTS

PART I: 2012-2013

PART II: 2020

Part I

2012-2013

PREFACE

My name was Silvia Milescu. I was born in Romania on July 14, 1990 and my heart stopped beating in California on August 2, 2013. I was twenty-three years old.

It is said people forget everything that happened to them before the age of two. But my first memory goes back even further, to the time when my mom was still driving me around in a baby carriage. We were going along Lacul Tei Boulevard, not far from the center of Bucharest, and I was just falling asleep when I heard a noise. I had no idea what it was, but I already knew those sounds – hoofs clapping, harness rattling, snorting – belonged to an animal that would play an important role in my life. I was so anxious to see what it was that my mom had to lift me up. And there was a pair of big draft horses with long thick manes, thick necks and strong legs, pulling a wagon. I started to whoop with joy, stretching out my little hands in an attempt to touch those huge animals, to climb on them, to ride them…

And as I grew up, nothing changed. In kindergarten, I only drew pictures of horses and, when I was old enough, I began to help out at a local horse place called Western Ranch. I rode whenever I got my dad to pay for a lesson, which wasn't very often. We weren't rich. My dad was a cook at the Phoenicia Grand Hotel and my mom worked in a boutique.

So when I was fifteen, I was delighted to find a horse owner who let me ride his three year old filly for free. Who wasn't very happy about it, though, was my mom. I was her only child, and she always worried about me a lot. She claimed I didn't have enough riding skills to handle such a young horse. Of course she was right, and I ended up in hospital after only a few days when the filly shied in canter. I broke both long bones in my right forearm and doctors had to put wires in them, so they would stay in place and grow back together right. I had a cast for two months.

Even though my arm healed nicely, I had to promise my mom I would never ride again. Naturally, I broke my promise as soon as I could hold the reins. I loved my mom deeply, but as time passed, I became really good at tormenting her.

At university I started to travel. I spent two summers in England as an au-pair, and one semester on a student exchange program in Lisbon. After graduation, my mom hoped I would finally settle down, so it was a big shock for her to hear I was leaving again for the whole year. I was heading to the United States as an au-pair to try life in the land of unlimited possibilities.

Before my departure my mom cried a lot. I thought she had already gotten used to my living abroad, but this time, it was different. Six thousand miles and the Atlantic Ocean would divide us, and as neither of my parents had ever flown, nor did they speak any English, it would be practically impossible for them to come if something happened to me. My mom simply hated the idea I would be completely on my own. Or maybe, somewhere deep in her heart, she already felt I wouldn't be coming back and she would never see me again.

Nevertheless, she knew very well that trying to persuade me to stay home would have been a waste of time. I had always been quite stubborn, and when I set my mind on something, no one could talk me out of it.

1

Mount Diablo

My host family, the Bells, were from Contra Costa County, California. Peter and Amanda Bell lived at the foot of Mount Diablo near Clayton, about an hour's drive from San Francisco. Peter worked in the city as a project manager at Wells Fargo Bank and Amanda was a real estate agent. They had three boys – five-year old Christopher, seven-year old Sean and Jacob, who was going to be eleven soon. In England, I took care of three sweet little girls, so I had no idea what I would do with the boys, but I knew the West Coast was the right place for me. Everything pulled me there – the weather, the countryside, the cowboys and, of course, horses and western riding. That's why I didn't hesitate a minute to become the Bells' seventh and last au-pair.

The journey to California was long and demanding, and when I woke up in the Bells' house for the first time, I hadn't the slightest idea where I was. *At home in Romania? On Manhattan where I took my au-pair training?* There was already light outside and rays of the sun were sneaking into the room through the closed venetian blinds, but I didn't recognize my surroundings at all. I had to think really hard before I realized that early that morning, the Bells drove me to their place, and the room I was in was to be mine for the next twelve months. It took me a few more minutes to figure out what day it was and I came to a conclusion it had to be Friday. I would never have believed jet leg could be so bad.

The flight to San Francisco was beautiful, though. It was a night one, so once we got out of the storm clouds, we had a great view of the huge clusters of lights that were the big cities below us. We landed in San Francisco at two in the morning, which was when I met the Bells for the first time. They were waiting for me in the arrival lounge – all of them!

Oh no, the boys will get almost no sleep because of me! I thought, feeling a bit guilty.

The boys were rather shy, but Peter and Amanda greeted me warmly and asked about my journey. They looked exactly like the photo I had. Peter was tall with brown hair and blue eyes. He wore glasses and was fairly good-looking. Amanda was quite short and had short blond hair. She was tanned and very pretty. All three boys were cute, but Christopher, the youngest one, was the most adorable. He had dark hair and big brown eyes, and he still kept his baby plumpness. He was unbelievably sweet.

I sat up in my huge queen-size bed and was staring at the green bankers lamp on my new desk. In the last six days, I had crossed at least ten time zones, so it was hard to say what my biological clock would consider the lesser evil – to get up or to go back to sleep.

Eventually, I decided to get out of the bed and explore my new home. On the bedside table I found a welcome card from the previous au-pair. *How nice of her!* Her name was Erika and she was from Germany. I knew from Amanda she hadn't been very happy living out there on the mountain, and I hoped I would make some friends so I wouldn't feel as isolated and lonely as she did.

The room was big and light. I tried the door on the other side of the bed and couldn't believe my eyes. *My own bathroom!* What amazed me even more was the big mirror above the sink. It was surrounded by tens of bulbs and when I saw my reflection, I felt like a movie star. You wouldn't find anything like that in Romania.

When I'd had enough of my gorgeous bathroom, I opened the other door that led to the hall and, from how quiet it was, concluded I was alone in the house. I vaguely remembered Amanda telling me last night in the car that they would let me sleep in. I tried the doors next to my room and they both led into the boys' rooms. To my surprise, they had their own bathrooms as well. *How many bathrooms do they have?!*

I went down the hall and it took me to the heart of the house that consisted of an open dining room with a big solid wood dining table and a large entrance hall with a sitting area, a fireplace, and a piano. *Wow, the house is so big!* To the left of the dining room there was a staircase to the first floor and I could see there were two more doors upstairs. I didn't go there, assuming they were Peter and Amanda's bedroom and study.

The dining room led to the kitchen that opened into a spacious family room with another fireplace. Amanda had told me to help myself to any food I found but I had no thoughts of eating. I opened the vertical blinds by the kitchen table and looked out through the glass sliding door. It led onto a patio and a small back garden surrounded by a low wall. Higher up the mountain, I could see the closest corner of a wooden structure that looked like a covered riding arena. My heart skipped a beat. *Neighbors with horses?!*

I stepped outside into the midday heat and was immediately blinded by the sun. I narrowed my eyes and went for a stroll through the garden. Passing some blooming bushes, I came across the tiniest bird I had ever seen. The hummingbird was hovering in mid-air, flapping his wings rapidly while drinking nectar from a blossom. I had never witnessed anything so beautiful.

I was really tempted to climb up the mountain to find out something about the horses, but I decided to wait for the Bells to ask them about our neighbors first. Instead, I walked around the house to the front yard.

As I came round the corner of the house, I saw a red Honda Odyssey parked in front of the garage. I knew it would be my car for the year because Peter and Amanda had gone to work in their cars. That was one of the great things about being an au-pair in the States – you got a car to drive the kids around.

In Romania, I could only dream of driving. I'd had my driver's license since I was eighteen, but my father always had some excuse ready for why I couldn't drive his old Volkswagen Passat. The truth was I didn't really need to drive in Bucharest as there was a very good public transport system there. But for me, it was a sign of personal freedom to be able to go wherever whenever I wanted.

I left the house behind and walked down the tarmac driveway. The slope was gentle at first, but soon it became very steep. Through the trees, I could see the road below and the golden hills of California stretching to the horizon. I suddenly realized there was nowhere to go. I was literally stuck on the mountain! I turned back and got a postcard view of the Bells' big pale blue house surrounded by yellow grass and dark green oak trees. *Wow, what a beautiful home they have,* I thought.

On the left side of the house where I hadn't been yet, I noticed some movement in a pen with a shed. I came closer and found three miniature goats. They were brown with white and black markings, and had long, drooping ears. They were so cute. *You must belong to the boys,* I thought and made a mental note to ask them what their names were.

When Amanda and the boys returned home, I was in the middle of unpacking my things.

"Did you find your room okay?" she asked after we greeted.

"More than that, it's great! And the bathroom – it's absolutely fantastic!" I exclaimed.

"I'm glad to hear that," Amanda said smiling, and asked me if I got enough sleep.

"Yes, I am fine, thank you." Actually, it was going to take a few more nights of good sleep to feel fine, but she didn't need to know that.

"Okay, so I'll make dinner now and we can talk more during the meal," Amanda said finally and sent the boys, who were eyeing me curiously, to take their stuff to their rooms.

Well, that wasn't so bad, I thought with relief. The first days in a new host family were always a little awkward.

By the time dinner was served, Peter had arrived home from work too. The food was delicious. We had steak with peas, corn and baby carrots, potatoes and salad. I was glad for the vegetables but in fact, I was so hungry I would have been grateful for any food.

Peter was drinking Ursus, the Romanian beer I brought him as a present – a whole carton of it. He said it was interesting, which probably meant he didn't much like its taste. For Amanda, I had a traditional Romanian pottery plate (it was more compact than a vase) and each of the boys got a carved wooden toy and some Romanian candies. They seemed to like them, though. I knew my small gifts were dumb, but my budget was limited and I was told by the agency to bring something typically Romanian.

It didn't take long for the questioning to begin. Surprisingly, it was Jacob, the oldest boy, who started.

"Do you live in a big city?"

"Yes, Bucharest is the largest city in Romania," I replied. "But it's not as big as New York or San Francisco, and we have no skyscrapers there."

"Bucharest is the capital city of Romania and has almost 2 million inhabitants," Peter filled in.

Wow! I was impressed. He evidently did his homework.

"Does your family have a big house?" Jacob asked next.

"We live in an apartment. I have always thought it big enough, but compared to your house," I looked around their huge hall, "it's quite small."

Both Peter and Amanda laughed.

Then Jacob wanted to know whether we had any pets.

"We have a dachshund called Danny."

"A sausage dog," Peter explained to the boys.

"He is black with brown markings, and he is the cutest and most stubborn dog in the world," I added. I was exaggerating, but only a bit.

"Do you have TV in Romania?" Sean asked.

I replied that we did watch TV in Romania as well.

"And do you have Harry Potter?" Christopher spoke for the first time.

"Of course, we do! In fact, I am a big fan of Harry Potter. I've read all the books and seen all eight movies."

My answer seemed to assure him I was suitable for the job.

"Do you play baseball in Romania?" Jacob continued his questioning.

"Not really. Football, I mean soccer, is quite popular there and we also play basketball. But I played softball several times in high school."

"That's great! You can join our baseball team," Peter suggested.

"Oh, I don't think that would be a good idea," I said fast. "You wouldn't want me on your team. I am terrible with a ball." Well, that wasn't exactly true. In fact, I used to be quite good at volleyball and basketball, but I still remembered how bored I was waiting for my turn to play when we played softball.

To change the topic, I asked about the arena I had seen up the mountain.

"It's Theresa's," Peter said. "She lives in the house behind it."

"So she has horses?" I asked with hope.

"She boards horses from time to time. But at the moment, she has just two ponies. Those are hers," Amanda explained.

What a pity! A riding arena without horses. I had nothing against ponies but since I couldn't ride them, they simply didn't count.

"We'll take you up there tomorrow to introduce you to Theresa," Peter said and Amanda added, "You'll like her, she's a sweet lady."

"And on Sunday," Peter continued, "you're going to test drive the Honda. We'll go to Clayton and I'll show you where you will be dropping the kids off for school."

"Okay," I said, managing a small smile.

I was looking forward to driving that nice big red car, but at the same time, I was a bit worried. Before my departure, I took driving lessons to brush up my skills, but it wasn't enough to make feel comfortable behind the wheel. The fact that I was going to drive an automatic car in a foreign country didn't help either.

"Have you already seen our pets?" Sean interrupted my train of thoughts.

"Do you mean your miniature goats?" I asked.

He nodded.

"Yes, I've already had the pleasure. They're the cutest goats I have ever seen!"

"Mine is called Brownie, she is the darkest one," Christopher said enthusiastically. It seemed I had finally earned his trust.

"You can feed them with us after dinner," Sean suggested.

For dessert we had the most delicious ice cream I had ever eaten – cookies and cream flavor. It was so good that it should have been illegal. While helping myself to a second scoop, I sadly realized I would have to watch my figure again. I had the same problem in England. All those great new tastes made me eat more. In Portugal, though, it was different. I had to buy food there myself, and the more I saved on it, the more I could spend on traveling.

After dinner, while I was helping Amanda load the dishwasher, I looked out the kitchen window and noticed the sun had already set over Mt. Diablo and our side of the mountain was covered by shade. My eyes focused on some dark shadows under the oak tree not far from the house and what didn't I see – a herd of more than ten deer.

"There are deer outside!" I exclaimed.

"Yep, I know," Amanda said. "They live here with us. Since nobody hunts them here, they aren't afraid of people. They won't let you come too close, though."

Peter joined in our conversation from the living room. "Coyotes and mountain lions live on the mountain as well. But you won't see them during the day, and they wouldn't come as close to the house, either."

"And a legend says that a phantom black panther can be seen on the mountain slopes," Amanda said in a spooky voice.

"Wow, real wilderness you have here! One should be afraid to go outside," I said smiling but thinking I should better stay home after dark. *Well, at least they don't have bears and wolves here.*

"Unless you go hiking alone at night, you are pretty safe."

Peter sounded reassuringly, so I decided not to worry. But the phantom black panther reminded me of what I had been wanting to ask them since I had read their first email.

"Why is the mountain called Mount Diablo?"

"Well, it got its name at a time when this all around was still Indian land, and there were clashes between Indians and Spanish soldiers," Peter began. "There are several versions of the story. One of them is that in the middle of a battle, a shaman appeared on the top of the mountain dressed in feathers. The Spanish ran away thinking they saw the Devil."

"And the mountain glows red at sunset," Amanda added in that spooky voice of hers.

I smiled at her. Actually, all that didn't even come close to what I had imagined – unexplained deaths, people gone missing, or some Devil worshiping sect conducting satanic rituals on the top of the mountain. Their explanations were much more acceptable.

The boys entered the kitchen with a bowl of carrots and apples.

"Silvia, we are going to feed the goats. Are you coming with us?" Jacob asked.

"I wouldn't miss it for the world!" I said and we went outside together.

Jacob's goat was called Nibbler, for it liked to nibble on clothes, and Sean's was Star, because it had a small white patch on its forehead.

Peter came along, bringing the goats fresh water.

"It's nice the boys have pets they can take care of," I remarked.

Peter smiled. "They're not just pets, they're also very useful. We let them loose when we are at home and they graze on the grass and dry oak leaves around the house. They are our four-legged lawn mowers."

"You see, the danger of fire is quite high during the dry season, so we want to keep the grass short," he explained.

I looked around and realized how dry everything was. It was the beginning of September and it seemed it hadn't rained for weeks. If a fire broke out, it would spread in no time.

On Saturday afternoon we went to visit Theresa. Instead of walking all the way down to the road and up her driveway, which ran alongside the Bells', we climbed to the arena across the rough terrain of the mountain. When we got there, a lady in her mid-forties emerged from a shed behind it. She was fairly tall and tanned with long blond hair pulled back in a ponytail.

"Hello there! How nice of you to visit your old neighbor!" she greeted us warmly.

Then she looked at me. "And you must be the new au-pair!"

"Theresa, this is Silvia. Silvia, this is our dear neighbor Theresa," Peter introduced us.

"Nice to meet you," Theresa said and shook my hand firmly.

"Come on in and I'll make you some lemonade," she gestured towards her house. It was yellow with white trim and much smaller than the Bells'.

The boys wanted to explore the arena instead, and as it was exactly what I desired too, I suggested I would stay with the kids and we would join them later.

We entered the arena through the open gate and found two ponies standing together in a corner, looking at us warily. The adult one, quite small even for a pony, was a pitch-black mare, and the other one was only a few months old foal. It had a beige, velvety fur coat with a highlighted dark mane and black lines around its eyes. It was very handsome.

"That's Black Beauty and her baby Spirit," Jacob informed me.

As we came closer, the ponies decided they wouldn't stand the intruders any longer and ran away through the open gate. They kept running about the dusty grounds outside while the boys were scampering around in the arena. The resemblance was quite striking.

It was a fine riding arena with a sand surface surrounded by about one-meter high wooden sidewalls. I imagined how great it would be to ride a horse there. *Stop dreaming, Silvia! There aren't any horses!*

To the right of the entrance, at the short side of the arena, there were two boxes and one slightly bigger stall, with a hay storage loft overhead, which was evidently occupied by the ponies. Each of the empty boxes led into a small paddock in front of the arena. It was a perfect horse facility in a wrong place – nice stalls, great equestrian arena, but no open space for riding and no pasture.

Half an hour later, we were all in Theresa's house drinking refreshing lemonade with ice and eating cake. Theresa spoke about her store and how busy she had been lately. She was a widow. Her husband left her an animal feed store in Livermore, and although she had two part-time employees, the run of the business lay only on her shoulders.

Theresa's husband was a horseman, and when Peter mentioned I liked horses and rode as well, it caught Theresa's attention.

"Really? In that case, I might have a job for you!"

I was all ears. Anything connected with horses was the right job for me.

"I need somebody to take care of the ponies. You know, groom them, let them out, clean the stall..., and Black Beauty also needs some exercise. I've quite neglected her lately."

"No problem. I'll be more than happy to help you out," I said, trying to sound more enthusiastic than I really felt. For a second, I hoped I would be working with real horses.

"I suppose you won't have much time during the week, but I would really appreciate if you could come at least on weekends."

"If you won't mind Silvia taking the boys with her, they can also come during the week," Amanda suggested. "They didn't come here with Erika because she was afraid of the ponies."

How can anyone be afraid of ponies? I wondered.

"That would be great!" Theresa exclaimed excitedly.

And we had a deal!

When we were leaving Theresa's house, Peter decided they would take me to an abandoned cottage further up the mountain. We set out down Theresa's driveway and, after a few yards, came across another driveway which led away from her place. We continued along it, and in less than fifteen minutes arrived at an old cottage with a shabby wooden shed next to it. It wasn't even four o'clock yet, but the sun had already gone over the mountain, casting a shadow upon the place and making it look even spookier.

Amanda told me that the old man who had lived there died two years earlier, and it had been on the market since then. No wonder nobody wanted to buy it.

"The cottage is over one hundred years old. I was inside once with my colleague realtor and it has a really big wine cellar," she added.

I shivered, imagining what other uses a big cellar could have in a place like that.

Behind the cottage started a trail which led further up the mountain. It was quite steep and rocky and overgrown with weeds. As Peter had never taken that one before, he wanted to explore it, but the climb was too hard so we gave up after about five hundred meters and turned back.

When we arrived home, I was starving and couldn't wait for dinner. Amanda fixed it quite fast and it was delicious again. *Oh no, I'm eating like a horse here!*

Because Amanda was opening a house for sale on Sunday, Peter took the boys with us on my test drive, which made me even more nervous.

I managed to start the Honda on the first attempt and slowly started to drive down the Bells' driveway. It was really steep.

"If you don't want to wreck the brakes soon, stop pressing down on the brake pedal all the time. You must brake in intervals," Peter advised me.

Good to know! I will definitely need my brakes here!

At the bottom of the mountain, I turned onto Morgan Territory Road. We passed big houses and horse ranches scattered along it, with Mount Diablo on our left and beautiful rounded golden-brown hills on the right. Peter told me to make another turn and in less than fifteen minutes, we were entering Clayton. I liked driving the Honda. The driver's seat was higher above the ground than in the cars I had driven before, which gave me a better view of the road. So far everything was going great.

And then we came to the first intersection with traffic lights. As the light turned red, I started slowing down to stop at the lights, but suddenly Peter cried out, "Stooooop!!!"

Shocked, I stopped abruptly. But when I looked around, I knew immediately what had happened – I was nearly in the middle of the intersection! The traffic lights weren't mounted at the stop line, like I was used to from Europe, but at the far side of the intersection. We were lucky there were no cars coming from the other directions at the time.

Shit! I screwed that up! I thought when I looked back at the boys and saw their startled faces.

Trying to pull myself together, I faced Peter who was staring at me questioningly, his eyes wide with horror.

"I am so, so sorry!" I apologized and explained that in Europe, we stopped at the lights.

"Well, at least we didn't crash." stated Peter sounding much calmer. He took it fairly well.

I set the car in motion again and we continued to Mt. Diablo Elementary School. Peter showed me the drop-off area and also where to park when picking up the boys after school. *Parallel parking. Great!*

Our next stop was a grocery store. On the way there, we came across a four-way stop and this time Peter explained the local rules to me before we got there. I found it quite funny. It definitely wouldn't work in Europe, as every driver would claim he had been there first.

I parked neatly in the parking lot in front of Safeway, quite satisfied with my driving after the incident, but Peter raised his eyebrows in disbelief.

What have I done now?!

"Did you just brake with your left foot?" he asked.

Jesus! I really did.

I managed a weak smile. "I'm not used to a car with an automatic transmission."

Peter hesitated a bit and then said gravely, "Silvia, I thought you were an experienced driver."

"Did you?" I asked sounding surprised. I was quite confused.

"You said you had been driving for four years!"

He was referring to our only phone conversation before I came to the States. He asked me how long I've had my driver's license and I answered four years.

It suddenly made sense. *God, I was stupid! What was I thinking of? Of course they wanted an experienced driver for their sons!*

I couldn't look Peter in the eyes. Staring at the logo on the steering wheel, I slowly explained the misunderstanding. "I just said I've had my driver's license for four years, not that I had been driving the whole time."

In the States, it probably meant the same, but when you were a woman in Romania, those were two totally different things.

We sat quietly for a while, both staring ahead of us.

"Don't worry about it," Peter said finally. "You will drive here a lot and you will become an experienced driver soon."

I was so relieved to hear that! For a moment, I was really scared they would send me back home.

We got some groceries and Peter helped me open my bank account at the local subsidiary of Wells Fargo. I liked the bank immediately, and not only because they had horses in their logo. Peter mentioned I was going to take English classes and they automatically provided me with a student account which was free of charge. I couldn't see that happening in any bank in Romania.

I set off for home in a good mood. Because I already knew where I was going, I also knew there would be no more unpleasant surprises. Most of the way we had a great view at

Mount Diablo. It was vast and massive and, with its several peaks, it looked rather like a small mountain range.

When I finally pulled up in front of the Bells' garage, relieved I had made it, I realized I was starving again. It must have been the air there or something.

2

Halloween

I liked my new life in California a lot. The Bells were nice and the boys weren't as difficult as I had feared. They did have their moments though, and sometimes they were quite a handful. Especially Sean and Christopher, being the best of friends one moment and the worst enemies the next. They knew how to start a good fight.

My daily routine was great, especially because I did so much driving that it was like a dream come true. At ten in the morning, I drove Christopher to kindergarten and then I drove to Concord, the nearby town where my school was.

I took English classes for immigrants at the Loma Vista Adult Center. I was the only one from Romania there (you don't meet many Romanians in California) and it was the best language course I had ever visited. Instead of going through boring grammar and vocabulary, we learned about the past fifty years of American cultural history, analyzed songs and learned slang and idioms from particular decades. We had two teachers at the same time, Beth and Jane, and they spoke about important events in such an interesting and animated way, it was like traveling back in time.

From my English class I drove back to Clayton and, since I still had some time before picking the boys up, I did some shopping or stopped at Starbucks or at the Clayton library.

Most of the afternoons we either stayed home or went to Theresa's. The boys loved it there (and so did I), so I tried to make it to the ponies at least twice a week. We groomed them and cleaned the stalls and the arena. The boys could be very helpful when they wanted, but often they were too busy running around playing games.

Exercising Black Beauty wasn't easy because she wasn't at all cooperative. While I was longeing her, she kept bucking and kicking her back feet in the direction of the whip, and sometimes even at me. She should have been called Little Black Devil. After several tries, I gave that up and, having found a small saddle and a child-size helmet in the tack room, began to walk her around the arena with Sean or Jacob on her back. She didn't like that much either, but at least she didn't buck. Nevertheless, I didn't trust her and stayed alert, never loosening my grip on the rains. Christopher begged me to let him ride too, but I didn't dare to put him on such an unreliable pony. He was only five and if she did something, he would be down before he knew it.

Spirit was still too young for training and, because I had no experience with foals anyway, I only introduced him to a halter and we practiced walking on a lead rope. He was much more cooperative than his mother. One day he was going to make a great pony for some kid and I hoped it would be Christopher.

Theresa insisted on paying me for taking care of the ponies and, even though I tried to argue about it at first, I was glad in the end. Considering I spent almost nothing on food and didn't have to pay rent, my nearly two-hundred-dollar weekly allowance wasn't bad, but I could always use some extra money for gas or buying some clothes. Since the boys helped me, I paid them their shares and they were excited about making money.

I watched the boys until Amanda or Peter arrived in the evening, and then we had dinner. I was really glad I wasn't expected to make it because, unlike my father, I was no great cook and I would have been afraid they wouldn't like my cooking. I only made simple meals for the boys, like macaroni and cheese or tuna casserole, and I was fine with that. Usually, it was Amanda's job to make dinner, but when Peter occasionally cooked, it was very good as well.

I cooked dinner only once when Peter asked me to make a traditional Romanian meal for them. I think he considered it to be a part of our cultural exchange. I made Sarmale, which are cabbage rolls stuffed with ground pork, rice, sauerkraut, and tomatoes. I didn't have the nerve to make polenta as a side dish, so I made mashed potatoes instead. The outcome of my effort wasn't that bad, but the Bells didn't eat much of it and Peter never asked me to cook for them again.

My eating habits luckily returned to normal soon, but the food there was so caloric that I had to watch my figure anyway. So I skipped dinner twice a week and instead got some exercise at the Clayton Fitness Center. I liked it there. The staff was friendly and it was well equipped.

When I was returning home from the gym, it was already dark and I had to watch out for the deer. There was often a herd of them in the middle of our driveway and I had to stop and blow the horn to get them moving. They were quite fearless.

As I didn't watch the boys on weekends, I spent almost every Saturday in San Francisco. The Bells didn't want me to drive the Honda on freeways, which was totally understandable due to my lack of driving experience, so I left the car in Pleasant Hill and went by BART, a train that goes underground somewhere in Oakland and continues to San Francisco through the tunnel built on the bottom of San Francisco Bay.

I grew fond of the city immediately for it strongly reminded me of my beloved Lisbon. They had so much in common – the bay, the hills, the cable cars, and, above all, their glorious bridges (Lisbon's 25 de Abril Bridge looked very much like the Golden Gate).

I visited all the famous places I had heard of, like Russian Hill with the most crooked street in the world, Telegraph Hill with its Coit Tower and pretty views, bustling Chinatown, beautiful Golden Gate Park, and many others. I also visited playful sea lions on Pier 39 several times. There were hundreds of them and it was so much fun watching them banter noisily and crawl over each other on numerous wooden pallets, or play in the water.

On the Saturday before Halloween, I went to San Francisco as usual, but this time I was meeting the other au-pairs there, because the agency had organized an Alcatraz trip for us. Visiting the famous prison was quite an experience. Even San Francisco looked different from the Rock. It was covered in mist and with the mass of gray water in the foreground looked much gloomier and more dramatic than usual.

On the ferry back to the mainland, I chatted with a Polish girl called Irena and a Slovak girl, Marika. They knew each other well and spent their free time together as Irena lived in Walnut Creek and Marika close by in Pleasant Hill. They were planning to go to the Castro on Halloween and offered me to join them.

"Aren't you working?" I asked instead of answering. Halloween was on Wednesday and I was working as usual.

"We arranged it with our host families," Marika explained. "The parade starts in the evening anyway."

"I can ask Peter and Amanda but I usually watch the boys till six, and then it would be too late to go to San Francisco." I didn't want to come home in the morning and be dead-tired the whole of Thursday.

"Ask them and you'll see," Irena suggested. "Trust me. You don't want to miss it while you are here!"

She was a bit bossy, but very persuasive. I was suddenly quite tempted to go.

That evening, I told Amanda about other au-pairs going to the Castro and she was nearly as excited about it as the girls.

"Of course, you must go with them! You will have great fun!" she insisted, making the decision for me.

She even offered she would finish early and pick the boys up after school.

I had no excuse left. I was going to celebrate my first Halloween in San Francisco.

Getting ready for Halloween was great fun. I carved my first pumpkin and helped the boys with their own pumpkin scary faces. They looked great lit up on our front steps in the dark. We decorated the hall with the Halloween decorations we found in a box in the garage where we also discovered another box with Halloween costumes. The boys tried them all on, deciding which to wear to the costume parade at school. Jacob was going to be a pirate and Sean fit into Jacob's old Spiderman costume. Christopher was disappointed, though. He wanted to be a pumpkin, but it was one of the few costumes they didn't have.

On Halloween morning, Amanda had to leave for work early, so it was up to me to drive the boys to school. Jacob and Sean were already fully dressed in their costumes while Christopher was still in his pajamas. I was too busy with his brothers to get him changed, but when I took the same route two hours later, Christopher was wearing his brand-new pumpkin costume. He looked like a little pumpkin already, so dressed in the orange hat, pumpkin padded bodysuit and black sleeves and tights, he was absolutely adorable. I had to smile every time I glanced at him in the rearview mirror.

As I was meeting Irena and Marika later in the afternoon, I had enough time to go to my English class. We did idioms with death and bodies, and funny quizzes, and we had so much fun that I was glad I didn't skip it. And having my pockets full of candy for correct answers also made it worthwhile.

The girls were already waiting for me at the BART Station when I arrived in Pleasant Hill. Irena was dressed normally but Marika looked like a hard rocker. She wore an Ozzy Osbourne t-shirt, black jeans, and a black leather jacket. Her hairstyle was wild, and she had heavy black eye make-up and black nails. It hadn't occurred to me to wear a costume, so I was dressed in my black leather jacket with zippers on the sleeves, my favorite blue jeans, and new black ankle cowboy boots. With my long wavy hair hanging loose over my shoulders, I could be a rocker, too, but one who listened to soft rock.

When we came to San Francisco, it was already dark outside. We got off at Civic Centre and set off to the Castro on foot. The lit streets of San Francisco were already full of kids in costumes knocking on the doors of Victorian houses and shouting "trick or treat". The house doors were opening, and the homeowners were appearing with bowls full of candy. It was surreal; like watching a movie and being a part of it at the same time.

I was thinking of the boys. The Bells had gone to a Halloween party in Clayton, and I was pretty sure they were strolling the streets of their friends' neighborhood in their costumes at that time, too. Feeling bad about missing it, I left some candy under their pillows.

The Castro District wasn't far, and soon we were turning onto Market Street. Then I discovered what kind of neighborhood it was. I had never seen so many gays, lesbians and transvestites in my entire life! As it turned out, I was the only one who didn't know that the Castro was the largest gay neighborhood in the United States! Having quite a conservative upbringing, I was a bit shocked at first, but then I relaxed and, together with the girls, enjoyed the fun of commenting on the costumes that passed by us.

And the variety was amazing! Some costumes were quite funny, others were scary (especially dead corpses, vampires and other monsters), some glittered (mostly the transvestites' costumes), while others were nearly nonexistent (there was a couple of playboys who had on just tiny briefs and rabbit tails).

We were having a good time despite the growing crowd on the sidewalk, but then we came across a group of three young men dressed as superheroes. They were arguing about something and just as we were passing them, one of them, Hulk, raised his hand to punch Superman. Unfortunately, I was just behind him and he struck me in my head with his elbow. The blow knocked me off my feet and I fell to the ground.

Immediately, Irena and Marika, the drunk guys and several other people gathered around me to make sure I was OK. My head really hurt but I didn't want them to worry, so I stood up with some difficulty and assured them I was fine.

After walking several meters, I noticed my wrist was bleeding. I must have scratched it on the zipper of my jacket when I fell. Marika gave me a tissue to clean the wound and then another one to stop the bleeding. It was nothing, much worse was the head.

On the way back to Pleasant Hill, we didn't talk much. My head still hurt, so I closed my eyes and tried to get some rest knowing I would have to concentrate on driving soon. When I finally arrived home around one in the morning, I was dead tired. Peter and Amanda were already fast asleep, and I was really glad I didn't have to recount how my night in the Castro had gone.

In the evening, I called my mom at work. I just needed to hear her voice. We talked about everything and nothing, but I didn't dare mention last night. She would have freaked if I told her where I had been and what had happened to me. Even though my head was all right, she would have forced me to go to the hospital or worse, asked me to return home. And that was the last thing I wanted.

3

Old West Legacy

In November the rainy season began and the golden hills of California slowly started to turn green. It was raining all Saturday, so instead of going to San Francisco, I stayed home with the Bells. I occupied one of the two computers in the Bells living room to check my mail, which I hadn't done for a while, and then I searched the net for a place where I could go for a ride. I hadn't been riding for almost two months and it was high time to do something about it.

Christopher was leaning on my lap watching what I was doing while Jacob and Sean were fighting over the other computer, both wanting to play the same computer game. Amanda had to step in and make them take turns. In the end, I found a place in Walnut Creek where they offered commercial trail rides. Old West Legacy, as it was called, was located at the original Ford Ranch from the end of 19th century. The wranglers promised to take me on the trails of the Mt. Diablo Foothills where the "Old West" was still preserved. It sounded so good that I wasn't even discouraged by the price (they asked sixty dollars for a group trail ride), and called them immediately to book a ride. I was lucky, they had scheduled a group of four people for next Saturday and still had a couple of free horses.

I was so excited I would ride again that I arrived at the Ford Ranch half an hour earlier. It was at the very end of Castle Rock Road where houses were replaced by stables and paddocks with horses. I parked the car on a patch of dirt by a cluster of empty horse shelters, and got my old half chaps and helmet, which I had taken with me to the States, from the trunk.

As I was approaching an old wooden shed with a slanted roof, a scene from a western movie opened in front of me. There were seven horses tied up at a hitching post, a young man in western clothing was grooming one of them. Another cowboy appeared from the shed with a western saddle and bridle in his hands. A young woman with long blond hair was sitting in a chair by the entrance which was decorated with two cattle skulls and a pole with a big American flag. There was a little curly-haired girl running around a table. She was chasing a miniature rooster. On the table were three steaming metal cups and the smell of fresh coffee hit my nose. I died and went to heaven!

The cowboys greeted me warmly and said I was early. I didn't agree – I came just in time to see two real cowboys get horses ready for a trail ride! They were Anthony and his older brother Mike. Both were shorter than me and looked Latin American, but spoke without an accent. Mike introduced me his girlfriend Lucy and her daughter Samantha.

Since I was there first, Anthony let me pick a horse. I was thrilled. No one had ever let me choose a horse to ride before. Aside from Anthony's pretty palomino mare called Sandy and Mike's pinto Mustang Sugar, there were three chestnut Morgans and two Paint Horses. I didn't hesitate long. When would I get a chance to ride a Paint Horse in Europe? I chose a black and white mare called KitKat, and Mike told me it was Samantha's horse. *A kid's horse!* My instinct never failed me – I picked the nicest horse of them all.

I asked if I could tack-up KitKat myself and Mike told me to go ahead. He checked the saddle when I was done and was surprised I had placed and tightened it correctly. I explained that I had spent my childhood at Western ranch in Bucharest where they rode Western, too.

The group of the other four riders arrived shortly before eleven. They were two couples. I found it very romantic to go on a trail ride with a mate, however, I wasn't sorry to be there alone. I was finally able to ride again, which meant I could feel nothing but happiness.

Once everyone was on a horse, we set out along the trail that began across the road. Anthony went first, followed by the two couples, then KitKat and me, and Mike rode at the end. Anthony expertly opened the first of several gates for us and Mike closed them again when we passed. There must have been cattle grazing somewhere in the hills, but we didn't see any.

The pace was slow. Since the other paying customers were inexperienced riders, we could only walk. But not Sugar. She didn't know how to go slowly at all. She was dancing in place impatiently, wanting to run forward and spend all the energy she was overflowing with. She was like a time-bomb before an explosion. I was really glad I wasn't riding her. She would have given me the ride of my life, and when tired of my desperate bouncing on her back, she would have dumped me in a ditch. Even Mike, who was obviously an experienced rider, had his hands full. He had to turn her around on the spot in regular intervals to distract her and several times he parted with us to give her what she craved for – a good portion of running up and down the surrounding hills.

When Mike was around we chatted. He asked me how I had gotten to the States, and when I told him that I was an au-pair, he was quite interested to hear what it was like to live in a host family.

"And how about you? Were you born in California?" I asked him.

"We are from Costa Rica, but we came to the States with our parents many years ago when we were little boys." That explained their perfect English.

"Our father is a horseman too," he went on. "We have worked with horses all our lives."

I envied him. I had always wanted to be born into an equestrian family, but the only person in my family who had anything to do with horses was my great-grandfather who was a blacksmith.

Mike also said they were planning to move their horses. "The horse shelters get really muddy during the rainy season and it's bad for the horses' hooves. We're looking for a place with proper stables and a riding arena."

I told him about Theresa's almost empty arena up the mountain and he smiled.

"I guess no place is perfect! At least we have these beautiful trails here."

He was right, the scenery was so pretty! We left civilization behind, and rode through a valley between yellowish-green slopes speckled with small groups of oak trees. Hawks, the only visible inhabitants of that untouched piece of land, were circling high in the sky or hiding in the treetops, taking off when we disturbed them.

KitKat was a sweetheart and I enjoyed riding her a lot. She tested me a little in the beginning to see if I would let her graze, but once she saw I wouldn't, she gave in. The poor woman in front of me didn't make it so clear to her Morgan mare, and she fought with her the whole ride.

As we returned to the ranch, I dropped the reins and let KitKat graze on a strip of juicy grass. Then we untacked the horses and Mike showed me an old saloon that stood a bit apart near a huge cactus. It reminded me of the saloon they had at Western ranch, but this one was real and full of memories. Old dusty saddles and boots hung from the ceiling, and the walls were decorated with old photographs of cowboys and horses.

At that special place, Anthony gave me an offer I wouldn't have even dared to dream of. "If you want, you can help us with horses on weekends. I don't guarantee you'll get to ride every time, but if we have a free horse, we'll take you on the trails with us."

"Mike, are you serious?!" I exclaimed. I was so excited, that if I had been the hugging type, I would have surely given him a hug. Being the opposite, though, I just thanked him gratefully and we said goodbye on Sunday morning.

When I came home and told Peter and Amanda how lucky I had been, they were truly happy for me, and I had to promise the boys to take them to Ford Ranch with me sometime. In the evening, I also broke the news to my mom, but as she still didn't approve of my riding, she didn't take it half as well as the Bells. She sounded quite worried and I had to promise her to be careful.

Next weekend, like many others that followed, I spent both days at the ranch. On Saturday I went on a trail ride with three paying customers, but on Sunday I finally experienced some proper riding as my new friends took me for a "real" ride with six other cowboys. They showed me even more beautiful trails and we mostly trotted or cantered up long sweeping slopes. It was great and I felt fully alive again.

Mike's girlfriend Lucy, who was a second-grade teacher, was an even less experienced rider than me. But considering her Paint mare Missy was younger and livelier than good old KitKat, she did very well. It was Mike who brought her to horses and he had also been training her on Missy. They were a nice couple. Mike told me that since he started dating Lucy more than a year ago, they hadn't been apart for more than twelve hours. When I saw them together I thought, *this is what true love is about – being happy just to be together.*

When we were returning to the ranch more than two hours later, my behind was quite sore but I felt absolutely happy. It was right before Thanksgiving and I realized there were so many things I should be grateful for! At the top of the list was my own personal piece of the Old West where I could ride with cowboys on endless trails.

I had only one little problem – Anthony. He was seeking my company the whole day, telling me stories from his childhood and his riding beginnings. He even helped me into the saddle and rode next to me for most of the ride. I wouldn't have minded at all, but knowing he didn't have a girlfriend, I started to worry that for some strange reason, he had turned his attention to me.

On Thanksgiving Day, Peter's younger brother Mark came up from Los Angeles to celebrate the holiday with the Bells. Peter was happy to see him but a bit surprised. His brother, who was still single, usually spent Thanksgiving with their parents in San Diego.

Mark was in his late twenties, he was good looking like his brother, but he didn't wear glasses. Amanda told me that two years ago, he got together with their fifth au-pair Andrea from the Czech Republic, and that their relationship still lasted. *Wow!*

"Maybe you'll meet someone too while you're here," she teased me while I was helping her prepare Thanksgiving dinner. This time, I limited my cooking ambitions to peeling and cutting vegetables, but I was actually of some help when it came to pastries. We made three pies: an apple pie, a pumpkin pie and a pecan pie, which turned out to be the best pie in the world (served, of course, with vanilla ice cream).

"I doubt that," I replied honestly.

Being always in love with someone who didn't even know I existed or worse, who took me only as a friend, I had never had a boyfriend. There had been several boys who liked me, but I never felt the same way and always refused them.

The thought of Anthony crossed my mind. I hoped I was mistaken and he was just trying to be nice.

"How have they managed to keep their relationship going at such a long distance?" I asked to change the topic.

Amanda explained that Mark had made quite a few trips to Europe since Andrea returned back home, and so they saw each other every three or four months.

In the evening we brought all the dishes, including a good-size roast turkey, onto the festively set dining table. It was quite a feast! Even though we started to dine early that day, there was no chance we could finish all those goodies and we were going to have plenty of leftovers. Peter said a Thanksgiving prayer (a nice one), and we started to eat.

I was just helping myself to another portion of sweet potatoes when Mark made an announcement. "Andrea and I are getting married next year."

Wow, what news! It was hard to say who was more surprised – Peter or I. Amanda just smiled and, as I knew she stayed in touch with Andrea, I suspected she already knew what was coming.

Mark let the information sink in and continued, "The wedding will be on August 3 and we are going to live in the States."

My presence at that private family moment was a bit awkward, but when you are a live-in employee, you witness quite a lot from your employer's personal life. So when it came to hugging and words of best wishes, I just said, "Congratulations" and shook Mark's hand.

By the time the pies were served, planning was in full swing. The wedding was to take place in Prague, so Peter and Amanda decided to take two weeks off and use the opportunity to also visit other European cities like Vienna or Paris. And since it was going to be during summer vacation, they were thinking of taking the boys with them. At that point, I became a part of the planning as well. Because they were all going to be gone and I would have nothing to do, Amanda asked me if I could take my two-week vacation during that time.

"Sure, why not?" I agreed.

I hadn't made any travel plans yet, so it made no difference if I took my vacation in August or some other time. Although there were a few places I really wanted to visit, like the Grand Canyon, Las Vegas, and, of course, the Hawaiian Islands, I had no one to go with and I wasn't too eager to travel alone.

In December the trails became even more beautiful. Everything was so green and full of life. Santa came early that year and I got the best Christmas present I could have ever wished for two weeks before Christmas. An older couple bought an awfully expensive two-day horseback trip to Diablo Ranch, and Mike asked me to go with them as a second guide!

I couldn't believe my ears. "You want ME to be a guide?!"

"I would go myself, but I don't want to leave Lucy alone the whole weekend, and we also have two more trail rides to cover."

But Mike didn't need to explain anything to me – I would have sold my soul to the devil for a two-day ride. So I said yes, even though it meant spending the night with Anthony who was still awfully attentive to me. I was almost sure my suspicions were right by then, and I was already mentally preparing for an unpleasant talk.

We set out on Saturday before lunch. Anthony rode first on Sandy and I went last on KitKat. Since the couple were experienced riders, the pace was much quicker than with other paying customers. The trail we took soon became quite steep and rocky, and so I let KitKat pick the safest route. Being an experienced trail horse, she placed her feet expertly and carried me safely up the mountain.

I was in my element! I rode with purpose to a specific destination. It reminded me of the good old days when people used horses as a means of transport. I had always wanted to live back then (of course with all the modern conveniences and present-day level of healthcare).

It was the longest ride I had ever been on. We stopped only once to refresh ourselves and the horses and, after more than four hours, we were finally approaching a small group of farm buildings with white wooden fences. It was a charming place nestled in the very heart of Mt. Diablo, between its summit and an endless sea of the mountain foothills.

We were expected. An older man called Jack showed us the stables and the bathroom, and he also gave us some cookware from the kitchen. While the couple was exploring the ranch, I took care of the horses and Anthony got down to preparing dinner. When I joined him by the fire, the sun was already setting and the scenery looked even prettier. It was one of the most romantic places I had ever visited and I suddenly wished I was there with someone else.

"They do weddings here," Anthony said as if he could read my mind.

That wasn't a very safe topic for a conversation with him, so I switched to food.

"It smells good."

Maybe it was because I was starving but the canned beef stew he had heated tasted great.

The couple joined us for dinner and soon we were discussing our sleeping arrangements. As they preferred to spend the night in the barn, Anthony suggested that he and I stay outside by the fire. I wouldn't mind spending the night under the stars at all – Amanda lent me her thermal sleeping bag and one of their camping mats – but it meant staying alone with Anthony. Nevertheless, I wanted to give our customers some privacy, so I had no choice.

At first it was nice. I was cuddled in my sleeping bag, the fire was cracking and we were talking about life. But it didn't take long and the conversation took the direction I feared.

"Silvia, I've been wondering if you have a boyfriend in Romania?" Anthony asked out of blue.

Oh no, it's here!

"No, I don't," I replied bashfully. "If I had, I wouldn't be here in the States, but home with him. I take relationships quite seriously."

Anthony's eyes lit up with hope. He was getting ready to say something he wouldn't be able to take back and I didn't long to hear, so I added quickly, "That's why I decided not to go out with anyone while I'm here. I am returning back to Romania in a few months and I don't want to start a relationship that has no future." Well, that wasn't exactly true. I could always get married and stay in the States, like the Bells' au-pair number five was going to do, but I couldn't tell him that.

My words seemed to have the desired effect as Anthony's expression changed and he said rather sadly, "That's probably wise."

That didn't go so bad! I thought, relieved I didn't have to tell him directly that he was not my type. I knew it was shallow, but I could never date a guy who was shorter than me because I would feel like I was dating a younger brother. I needed a big strong man I could lean on.

My mom would have been so proud of me! I had just turned down my only admirer in the States. Although she was concerned I would stay single since I turned eighteen, she was far more concerned about me meeting someone in California and staying there for good.

The romantic atmosphere was suddenly gone, and neither Anthony nor I felt like talking anymore. We just made some arrangements for the morning and said good night.

For a little while, I lay in my sleeping bag with my eyes closed, worrying about Anthony's feelings, but soon a feeling of pure happiness spread through my whole body. *I made it! I conquered Mount Diablo on horseback.* Well, I hadn't been all the way to the summit, but I was close enough and had a strong feeling the mountain acknowledged my triumph, too.

In the morning, as we were getting the horses ready for the ride back, Anthony was more reserved than usual, but apart from that he acted quite normally. It was a big relief because I had honestly feared the previous night would ruin our friendship.

Riding down Mt. Diablo was slower and less comfortable than going up, but KitKat did great again. I just leaned slightly back, gave her control of her head and let her do her job. When we arrived at Ford Ranch after almost five hours, tired but in high spirits, Mike announced with a smile that I had just graduated from trail riding. I was really proud of myself, despite knowing that all the credit belonged to KitKat.

I called home that evening and it was my dad who answered the phone.

"Silvia, is that you?!" he exclaimed, happy to hear me again.

I was glad it was him, especially because we were on the same wavelength when it came to horses although he didn't ride. I shared with him all the details of my special ride up Mt. Diablo and he was almost as enthusiastic about it as I was.

"It must've been one hell of a ride!" he observed when I finished.

"How long did you go there?"

"Hm…something over two hours," I replied after some hesitation.

I hated lying to my father, but I just couldn't tell him that it was a two-day ride. Even though I was already grown-up and thousands of miles away from home, I was still his little girl and he wouldn't approve me spending a night with some cowboy, no matter how innocent it was.

"Two hours up, two hours down – that means you spent more than four hours in the saddle! That's your record!" my father exclaimed excitedly.

"Yeah dad, I had never done so much riding in one day." *Nor twice as much in two days!*

A week before Christmas, Amanda's parents, Carol and Jonathan, came to spend the holidays with the Bells. They flew in from Florida where they had bought a mobile house a few years ago. They spent winters there, but for the summer, to escape the hurricane season in Florida, they always moved back to their house in Maine where Amanda had grown up.

I had never met seniors who were so active and full of life. Every morning, Jonathan took his binoculars and went to watch hawks while Carol went for a jog. They talked a lot about their new life in Florida, and they were still full of impressions from their fall journey to Australia. The only downside of their great retirement lifestyle was that they didn't get to see their grandsons more than once or twice a year. Naturally, they wanted to enjoy the boys as much as possible while they were with them, so I didn't have much work during the winter break.

Jonathan told me many interesting things about Florida, among them the story of Florida grapefruits.

"They grow everywhere there, but most of them are left on the ground to rot since nobody eats them"

"Why?" I couldn't understand. I personally loved grapefruits, and if they grew where I lived, I would eat them every day.

But Jonathan explained it to me. "Florida has the highest population of seniors in the US, and most of them take pills for high cholesterol or high blood pressure. Since grapefruit juice interacts with these medicaments, most old people can't drink it."

The funny thing was that grapefruit juice itself was really good for lowering both high cholesterol and high blood pressure. That just confirmed what I already thought – people should take fewer pills and eat more healthy stuff.

On Saturday before Christmas, we all went on a Christmas hike together. We did the waterfall loop at Mt. Diablo State Park which was best to do in winter as you wouldn't find the waterfalls there during the dry season. It was a nice walk and it turned out the grandparents were in pretty good shape, too.

Although the house was full of people, I had never felt more homesick in my life as on that Christmas Eve. I really missed my family that day. It was my first Christmas away from home and it didn't feel like Christmas at all. I didn't help my father prepare Christmas dinner, didn't eat my favorite Christmas sweets and didn't go to the Christmas market in University Square with my mom and grandma. The market was illuminated with hundreds of thousands of lights, and I always got in the right Christmas mood there, strolling among the countless stalls with handicraft and food while listening to carol singers. And the weather wasn't right either. It was too warm and no chance of snow.

Opening presents on Christmas Day morning was one of the strangest things I had ever done. It should take place at night, when it is dark outside and the lights on the Christmas tree are on, not in broad daylight. I gave everyone something small and got an absolutely perfect present – a cowboy hat. I couldn't wait for my next ride!

Originally, I was supposed to celebrate New Year's Eve with Marika and Irena at a night club in San Francisco but, as I could hardly imagine myself spending the night at a dance party with a DJ, I gladly accepted Anthony's invitation to a New Year's Eve party at a nearby horse facility (of course after he had assured me he was asking me only as a friend).

Everybody was to bring something to eat and, after my success with the Thanksgiving pies, I decided I would bake again. I made cupcake-sized Savarinas, which are rum soaked cakes filled with whipped cream and decorated with strawberry jelly on top.

When I arrived at the party with a tray of them, the large room was already filling with people in western wear. I could have easily worn my new cowboy hat and wouldn't have looked strange at all. At least I wore my blue jeans and a checked shirt, so I fit in quite nicely.

There were plenty of new faces although I already knew some of the cowboys from the trails. "Crocodile Dundee" was there as well. I called him that, since Paul Hogan could have been his brother. He was in his sixties and looked just like him – tall, thin, fair-haired and tanned. He even had the same hat. He passed the Ford Ranch on his grey mare several times a day, usually in the company of two or three young female riders. Some people know how to enjoy retirement…

I found a spot for my Savarinas on a long table full of food and joined my friends from the ranch. Anthony introduced me to a lot of new people, but it was just too many names to remember. I only remembered Gus who was standing by a portable gas stove, stirring his big pot of meat balls with some red sauce. He insisted I had some and filled my plate. No wonder he was proud of his cooking – they were fantastic! When I went to get some brownies for dessert, I noticed to my surprise that my Savarinas were already gone. I wondered if it was because of the Christmas colors or because of the rum.

Later, karaoke started and I couldn't believe my ears. *Does everyone in the States know how to sing?* All the singers were very good which reminded me why I never sang in public. Anthony and Lucy didn't sing either, but Mike sang a duet with Samantha. It was a sweet performance. They sang some country song and Samantha, who had just turned eight, looked like a little country star, with her pretty long curly hair wearing a cowboy hat and high cowboy boots.

I had a great time despite it being my driest New Year's Eve since I had turned seventeen. There was plenty to drink, but because I was driving as usual and I would have never risked my precious driver's license, I stuck to Coke. I only had a tiny sip of champagne at midnight when we had a toast to the upcoming year 2013. I was so curious what wonderful adventures the new year would bring me for the rest of my stay in the States that I couldn't wait to start living it. If I only knew…

In January, we started the 70s in my English class, and from the very first day, I knew it was going to be my favorite decade. We talked about Woodstock and our teachers dressed up really stylishly for that. Beth came in a flowered dress and an afro wig, and Jane, who wore her long blond hair parted in the middle, put on bell-bottom trousers and a tight shirt. On top of that, they both wore platform shoes and were heavily decorated with beads. The moment I saw them, I finally fully understood the meaning of the word groovy.

Carol and Jonathan flew back to Florida a few days after the New Year and the house suddenly seemed empty. I missed their energy and optimistic approach to life. But Amanda's parents weren't the only ones who left us at the beginning of the new year – the deer disappeared as well. They stopped grazing around the house and I didn't run into them on our driveway anymore. Even Peter, who drove to work early and used to meet them almost every morning, didn't see a sign of them the whole month. He found it very strange since during the ten years they had lived there, the deer had never migrated. However, it looked that for some unfathomable reason, they left our side of the mountain that year.

At the beginning of February, Amanda came with some interesting news. She had heard from another realtor that somebody had rented the old cottage up Theresa's driveway. I wondered who would want to live in a place like that, but neither the Bells nor Theresa had ever seen anybody drive up there.

As it had been raining a lot the first two months of the year, the trails became so muddy that it was impossible to ride on them. So at the ranch, we were mostly grooming our small herd and cleaning the stalls. But the shelters got so muddy that removing the mud from the horses' hooves and legs became a never-ending battle – only a few moments after we put the horses back in, it looked like we didn't clean them at all. It was very frustrating and I finally understood why my friends were looking for better stables for their horses.

Nevertheless, it was a huge shock for me when Mike announced at the beginning of March that they found the place they had been looking for and were moving in two weeks.

"Where?!" I asked, already suspecting I wasn't going to like the answer.

"Near Fresno." Mike replied. "Lucy has already got a teaching job there."

My worst fears came true. It was almost a three-hour drive, which meant the end to my riding with the cowboys.

I was really sad about it but at the same time was happy for them. The equestrian center Mike and Anthony were going to work for was without any doubt a great horse facility. It had an indoor riding arena, two open-air arenas, comfortable stalls where they could board their horses for a good price, and large pastures. On top of that, they were going to teach western riding there like they always wanted. It seemed their dream had come true.

The following Sunday I went to Ford Ranch for the last time. Parting with KitKat after my last trail ride wasn't easy, but saying goodbye to my friends was even harder. Together with the Bells and Theresa, they were my closest people in the States. We hugged, said our best wishes and when I got in my car, I realized I would never see them again. That was it. My happy days at the ranch were over.

4

Peace

Spring came, the weather improved, and the baseball season began. Even Christopher started with baseball that year, so it made three trainings a week. If I found playing baseball boring, it was nothing compared to watching kids' baseball trainings. I always made sure to have something to read with me.

When we weren't at the baseball field, we passed our afternoons in the Mt. Diablo Elementary School multipurpose room where the school play rehearsals took place. They were doing Oliver Twist that year, and our little Jacob was going to be nobody less than the chief villain, Bill Sikes. All the kids were pretty good, but I liked the boy who played Oliver Twist and Jacob the most. I would have never believed he could be so convincing playing an evil character. He was quite scary rampaging on stage and being mean to poor Oliver and Nancy. Watching the rehearsals since November, I already knew all the lines and songs by heart (and so did Christopher and Sean), yet I still looked forward to the opening night at the beginning of May to see it in one piece and in full costume.

As Irena and Marika had already returned home and I suddenly had no program for the weekends, I returned to discovering the beauty of Northern California. I explored some other interesting places in San Francisco like the Presidio or the San Francisco Zoo, and with the Bells, I visited charming Old Sacramento and the Winchester Mystery House in San Jose. Although I was having a pretty good time, I still missed riding with the cowboys a lot.

"It's such a shame they had to move!" I complained to Theresa one Sunday at the end of April. It was a beautiful spring evening and we were sitting on Theresa's porch drinking wine like we used to in the fall.

Theresa gave me one of her secret smiles and said, "Every cloud has a silver lining." It almost sounded like she had something specific in mind.

We were talking until the night fell over Mt. Diablo, and when we realized how late it was, I went to round-up the ponies that were still running around loose. The lights on the arena illuminated a good part of Theresa's front yard, but it took me a while to find them because they had wandered off down the mountain. Nibbling contently on juicy grass by Theresa's driveway, they ignored my calling and I had to go get them.

Just before I reached them, I saw a car going down the driveway which led to the old cottage. The ponies lifted their heads up in unison and darted toward the arena like someone was chasing them. Curious to finally meet our new neighbors, I stayed where I was and watched the car approach the junction with Theresa's driveway. It was a dark pickup with two men inside. I didn't see them very well in the dark but could feel their chilling stares. As the car was passing me, a big fluffy dog's head popped up from the tailgate. It bared its sharp teeth and growled at me so menacingly that I shivered. I suddenly didn't feel safe out there anymore and hurried back to the arena.

When I joined Theresa, panting and out of breath, she was with the ponies, giving them grain.

"What happened to you?!" she asked worriedly.

"I think I've just met our new neighbors!" I replied in a shaky voice. Then I described my strange encounter to her.

The school play opening night was a big success. In full costume with decorations and proper lighting, it looked almost like a real play. In spite of being really nervous before his first performance in front of so many people, Jacob did a great job on stage, and so did the rest of the kids. I was really proud of them!

Theresa called me the following day in the morning which was quite unusual.

"Hi Silvia, what time do you drop Christopher off at kindergarten?" she asked me straight away.

"At half past ten, why?" I replied.

"I was wondering if you could come to my place afterwards. I want you to meet someone," Theresa explained.

"I have my English class – but if it's important, I can skip it. I could be at your place around eleven."

"Oh, please do. I'm sure you won't regret it. Okay, see you soon, bye!" And before I could ask who I was supposed to meet, she hung up.

I felt a bit guilty for skipping my English class, which I rarely did, but was also very curious. So I arrived at Clayton Elementary School earlier than usual, walked Christopher to the kindergarten playground and hurried back to Theresa's place. I remember it was one of the first hot days that year because I had the air-conditioning on. The car was the only place where I welcomed it. I liked hot weather, but a boiling car was too much even for me. It must have been around thirty degrees Celsius, but I didn't know it exactly since the weather forecast was in degrees Fahrenheit and I never bothered to find out how to convert them.

I parked my car at the end of Theresa's driveway next to an unfamiliar car and started walking towards the house, assuming they were inside. Soon I spotted Theresa in front of the tack shed talking to a man who was filling a bucket with water. He was tall, wore a white T-shirt and blue jeans, and a grizzled ponytail was sticking out the back of his black baseball cap. He couldn't have been more than forty-five.

Theresa greeted me with a smile and introduced us, "Walter, this is Silvia. Silvia, this is my old friend Walter. He brought his horses up here yesterday."

Horses?! Here?! I looked towards the arena and there were two horses' heads sticking out from the stalls.

"I'm just gonna bring them some water – do you wanna come along?" Walter asked me.

"I'd love to!" I said eagerly.

"I thought so," Walter smiled. "Theresa's already told me a few things about you..."

Walter lifted the two buckets of water with some difficulty, and when we walked across the arena towards the horses, I noticed he was limping on his right leg.

First, we came to a huge German warm-blooded stallion who was snorting nervously, trotting back and forth along the railing of his stall. He was brown with a round white mark on his forehead and white stockings, and his golden-brown eyes were showing too much white. I wasn't at all sure I wanted to ride that one.

"This is Mack," Walter said. "He doesn't like changes. It'll take him a while to get used to his new home."

He petted Mack on the neck and he calmed down immediately.

"He's like a child, always demanding my attention. But he loves me. I saved his life."

He gave him water and then we moved on to the other horse.

"This is Peace. His full name is Dash for Peace and Freedom. He is a three-quarter Thoroughbred and one-quarter Quarter Horse."

A beautiful dark brown gelding was eyeing me curiously with his big warm eye.

"He's fourteen," Walter went on. "When he was young, he ran races in Santa Rosa. He never came in worse than fifth but never won."

Peace looked like a nice horse, but as he was without any doubt a valuable animal, I had no reason to think his owner would let me ride him.

So I was absolutely astonished when, out of the blue, Walter said, "I've heard that you have no horse to ride at the moment. I wouldn't put you on Mack since I don't want you to end up in hospital, but I was thinking you could ride Peace."

I gave Theresa a grateful look. "I don't know what to say!"

"Great! Let's meet tonight at seven then, and you can test ride him," Walter suggested.

"Yes … yes, yes!!! I'll be here, exactly at seven!" I agreed excitedly.

In the evening, I came to Theresa's a bit early. I waited for Walter by the stalls, passing the time by petting Peace, who was nibbling gently on my sweatshirt, and watching Mack, who was still pacing nervously back and forth. He looked quite lost. Before I knew it, seven had passed but Walter wasn't there. At 7:30, I started to worry but stayed put. I wasn't going to give up so easily.

When Walter finally arrived, it was already quarter to eight. He apologized for being late and we got to work. We groomed Peace together and after Walter wrapped his legs in bandages, he saddled him up with a nice English saddle.

"All right, let's see what kind of a rider you are," he said when Peace was ready.

I was suddenly quite nervous. *Oh my, he is going to judge my riding!* I hadn't ridden English for over a year and knew I wouldn't be very good. But I realized it didn't matter. What was important was that I would ride again.

I mounted Peace and started walking around the ring. I couldn't believe it. After all those months I was finally riding in my beloved arena! Riding Peace was pure pleasure. He was a fine horse with fine movements, and I felt comfortable and safe on him. We trotted a lot and then we did big circles in canter. Peace was very responsive and I was content with myself thinking I wasn't such a bad rider after all. But that was the last time I felt satisfied with my riding. The next evening, Walter started to train me and I found out that I was doing almost everything wrong.

I knew right away Peace was no ordinary horse, but what I didn't know, was that Walter was no ordinary horse owner. He was a recognized dressage trainer and horse whisperer, and before his injury, an excellent dressage rider. He somehow managed to combine natural horsemanship and classical dressage and his name meant something in Californian equestrian circles.

Although Walter worked with horses for a living, Peace was the first horse he really owned. He found him eight years earlier in a racing stable south of San Francisco where he was training another horse. Peace was quite neglected then, because in spite of being fast, he didn't seem to have the heart of a winner. His owner had two other racing horses which he decided to focus on instead. Walter noticed Peace's graceful movements and, with the owner's consent, turned him into a dressage horse. They became a great pair and competed in dressage competitions all over California, always placing among the best. Three years later, the owner finally realized they belonged together and sold Peace to Walter for a price he could afford, which was much less than Peace's real value at that time.

But then came the injury and put an end to their nicely launched career. It happened while Walter was trying to calm down an injured stallion so the vet could approach it with a sedative injection. The frightened animal kicked him in his right knee with such force that it totally destroyed his knee cup and badly damaged both sides of his knee joint. He had to undergo total knee replacement surgery which was fairly successful, but he walked with some difficulty and due to the pain in his knee, he couldn't ride anymore.

In the years that followed, several dressage riders rode Peace, but none achieved such good results with him as his owner. Walter said it was because Peace didn't accept his new riders and didn't put his heart into the training with them.

Because of the handicap, Walter had to reduce his training activities and his regular employers gradually switched to other trainers. With two horses to feed and board, it didn't take long until he got into financial difficulties. So when his mother suddenly passed away that spring, he decided to return to Concord and move back into the house where he had grown-up. Since his father, who came from Holland and was also great with horses, died when Walter was a little boy, his mother was the only family he had.

As soon as Theresa learned her old friend was back and looking for a place for his horses, she offered to stable them in her arena. And since she had known him from way back when they were kids, she insisted on charging him only for feed and bedding. Needless to say, what a big favor she did me.

My first training began with Walter adjusting my stirrups.

"They are too long! I can't ride like this!" I protested, not feeling the usual support of my feet.

"Don't worry, you will get used to it," Walter assured me, sounding amused.

I didn't stop worrying but realized that complaining wouldn't get me anywhere.

Next, he started to arrange my body in a totally unnatural posture he called the correct seat.

"There! Now it looks much better," he said with satisfaction once he was done. "Try to stay like this all the time."

Although I was really trying, I kept slipping into my deep-rooted "wrong" seat. Walter wouldn't let me, though, reminding me constantly what I was supposed to be doing.

"Straighten up!"

"Shoulders down!"

"Elbows to the body!"

"Heels down!"

And when I thought I was finally doing everything right, he always found something else.

"Steady hands!"

"Head up!"

"Relax your pelvis!"

"Keep a contact with the reins!"

I couldn't help thinking it was impossible to concentrate on all those things at the same time. As if I didn't already feel miserable enough, he often let me stand in the stirrups for several strides and I, not having found my balance yet, kept falling back in the saddle.

Several trainings later, while I was still fighting with my seat, Walter introduced me to riding on a circle. "Whether you ride on the right or on the left hand, remember you need to slightly bend your horse so that his nose points inside. The simple rule is that you must always see the eye."

It sounded easy but, as it turned out, pulling on the inside rein didn't do the trick and I had to use my whole body to bend Peace correctly.

During the first several weeks, I felt like I was learning to ride all over again. I was quite frustrated and I often doubted I would ever get it right. But Walter was a good and patient teacher, and he never got tired of explaining to me, over and over again, what I should do and what effect it should have on Peace.

Sometimes I wondered why he was putting so much effort into training such a lost case, especially one who couldn't afford to pay him and was leaving in a few months. Walter saw it differently, though. He said he saw some potential in my riding and was also glad Peace got some exercise. He even claimed that Peace had accepted me as his rider, but I didn't believe him. *Why would Peace prefer my bouncing on his back and pulling on his mouth to the perfect riding skills of all those professional dressage riders?* It didn't make any sense.

To compensate Walter a bit, I offered to take care of Peace and Mack for him. Well, I did take care of Peace but as for Mack, I just mucked out his stall if I managed to lock him out in the outside pen or in the arena. He was really dangerous. In spite of Walter's warning, I approached him once and only narrowly escaped his kicks when he attacked me with his front legs.

Walter got Mack two years before for free. He was six then and had already hurt his owner several times. She became afraid of Mack and since nobody wanted to buy him, she was going to put him to sleep. In an attempt to save the horse, Walter started to work with him. Mack became attached to him, but even though they had good results together, he was still dangerous to everyone else. Walter had no choice – he could either take him or let him die.

As Mack didn't like being locked in his stall while I was riding Peace, his loud neighing often disturbed our training. It was a huge shame Walter couldn't ride him. He longed him from time to time, but that wasn't enough. The paddock was too small for him, so the only place where he could blow-off some steam was in the arena. I let him in there any time I could, but I always had some carrots or apples ready to get him back in his stall later. When I let Peace run freely in the arena, he was almost as wild as Mack, messing around and bucking like crazy, but as soon as I put the saddle on him, there wasn't a nicer horse.

We rode almost every night. Walter didn't mind the trainings being so late as he worked during the day anyway. He gave dressage lessons and trained a couple of horses at a horse club up the Clayton-side of the mountain. Since both Peter and Amanda were really busy at work (houses sell best in the spring and Peter was starting a new project at the bank), I wasn't usually off before seven. By the time Walter arrived, which was hardly ever before nine, I had the stalls cleaned and Peace groomed and saddled up. I also learned how to bandage his legs properly to prevent an injury. On my feet, I was wearing custom made English leather riding boots Theresa gave me. They belonged to her late husband and I found it weird to wear them first, but they fit me perfectly and riding in them was much more comfortable than in my old chaps and trainers.

When we started to ride it was already dark and so we had to turn-on the arena lights. The lighting was good, illuminating nearly the whole ring except for the far end that wasn't roofed. Although the arena was surrounded by pitch black darkness, interrupted only by the dim light coming from the Bells' living room, it didn't bother Peace and he fully concentrated on our training.

He spooked only once, not long after I started to ride him. We were just doing small circles in canter when Peace smelled something in the dark. He stopped abruptly, turning his head toward the mountain and taking in several deep breaths of the air. Then he went up on his hind legs and started to retreat while neighing wildly. I was lucky he didn't break my nose. Walter appeared by my side in no time and Peace came back down on the ground. He was still very nervous though, so Walter began to walk him round the arena. After several circles, he finally calmed down enough that we could go on with the training.

"It could have been a mountain lion," Walter said at the end of the lesson when I was practicing what he called "deep work". The principle of it was to let the horse chew the reins out of the rider's hands in walk so that his head came down and he could stretch his neck. It reminded me of letting horses graze at the ranch after the trail ride.

"People from the club said they saw one near Eagle Peak the other day," he went on.

"But Peter told me they wouldn't come too close to a house," I objected.

"Maybe he is hungry or he didn't smell us over the horse scent."

A hungry mountain lion lurking around the arena! I didn't like the idea at all, but it explained a lot. *Maybe it came here already during the winter and scared the deer away.*

"By the way, Peace just gave you another proof that he likes you," Walter added, interrupting my thoughts.

"Really?"

"When he stood up, he was protecting you with his body," he explained.

I was touched. *Maybe he does like me,* I thought while petting my knight in shining armor on his long neck.

That night Walter gave me a ride home. I was glad since I had no desire to meet the mountain lion in person while climbing down to the house.

After the incident, I started going to Theresa's by car. It was totally anti-environmental and took longer, but I didn't feel safe outside after dusk anymore and both Walter and the Bells insisted on it. Despite worrying a bit about my safety, Peter and Amanda took my night riding with Walter quite well. It would have been much harder to deal with my parents who knew I rode Peace, but had no idea I was returning home around eleven almost every night.

About a month after Walter started training me, the first results came. Not only was I used to my new seat, I even found it quite comfortable and felt a better connection with Peace. I could also stand in my stirrups for as long as I wanted because I was perfectly balanced. I learned how to post correctly in trot and keep my hands still. In canter, I finally managed to relax my pelvis, so instead of bouncing above the saddle like I used to, I followed Peace's movements, remaining in contact with saddle at all times. And what Walter appreciated the most, the inside bend had become an inseparable part of my riding.

It was a miracle! I had never ridden so well in my life. I was just at the beginning, though. The more I knew about riding, the more I realized there was still so much to learn. Especially after finding out what Peace was capable of.

Once, when I had the impression I was doing everything wrong again, Walter asked me to get off Peace and, despite the pain in his knee, showed me a half-pass in trot and a center pirouette. I was staring at him open-mouthed, totally in awe.

"He knows it all. You just need to know how to ask him to do it," he said, panting heavily, after bringing Peace to a halt. Then he dismounted slowly and grabbed his bad leg.

"Are you all right?" I asked worriedly.

"I'm fine!" he grumbled and hobbled to sit down on a bundle of straw while I replaced him in the saddle.

How I wished to ride like him! But I knew it would take me years. And I had just a few months...

5

Brian

I was standing in the darkness watching her ride as I had many times before. My faithful Ricky was lying motionless at my feet, taking in the smells and sounds that were surrounding us. It had become my favorite part of the night, something to look forward to, which I hadn't had in years. I was drawn to her like a moth to a flame.

When I first saw her, she was bleeding. It was Halloween night in the Castro, and since Alex and I decided not to take any chances, we stayed in our first-floor apartment on Market Street and watched the masses of people outside from the living room window. Suddenly, I saw a girl was knocked down to the ground by a drunk young man. When she got back to her feet, there was blood dripping from her wrist. Just a few drops, but it was enough for me to almost go insane. I had never had such an urge to drink from a human before.

Alex, who was standing next to me, was eyeing me with interest. "Go for it, Brian! There is nothing better. Believe me."

Alex was my companion, my teacher and my maker. Although he had a great pleasure in killing humans, he didn't do it to feed anymore. He killed only if he had to or if the person deserved it in his eyes. Since I have known him, he killed at least a dozen people: four of our landlords, five delivery men, a security guard in Vegas and two policemen.

But I wasn't like him. I could never kill a human if it wasn't absolutely necessary. So I just watched her disappear behind the corner, feeling relieved I would never see her again. I didn't know then that fate would bring us together again soon, only a few hundred yards from our new place on Mt. Diablo.

We were just leaving for a hunting trip up north when we saw a girl and two ponies by our driveway. I recognized her immediately – that beautiful face framed with a cascade of dark wavy hair, her cat-like eyes, the sweetness of her blood. The ponies fled to the neighbor's barn the moment they smelled us and she stayed standing there alone, watching us curiously with her full lips slightly parted. My good old Ricky must have really scared her because once we passed, she dashed to the barn almost as fast as the ponies.

I couldn't get her out of my head. I spent the following night circling the neighbor's place, hoping she would be there. She didn't show up that night though, nor the next two nights. But I didn't give up. If there was something I had, it was time. I continued watching our neighbor's place after dusk and a week later, luck finally came my way. I found her riding a horse in the arena on the other side of the barn. God, she looked good in the saddle! And she seemed so happy! I had always liked horses but never ridden one. It looked so easy when I watched her.

She wasn't alone. In the middle of the ring, there was a man sitting on a bundle of straw. He asked her how long she had been riding for and she answered that she had started when she was eight. She had a beautiful voice and spoke with an accent. I wondered who she was and why she was riding at night.

I found a spot behind an oak tree further up the mountain from where I had a good view of them and Ricky lay down at my feet. I took him almost everywhere with me as he didn't like to be alone with Alex. He was a bit annoyed that he couldn't see anything through the poison oak, but he knew he had to stay quiet.

Like him, I could hear every word the girl exchanged with the man, and soon got answers to most of my questions. Her name was Silvia and she was from Romania. After finishing university, she left for the States to become a live-in nanny in the family that lived in the house just below the arena. She worked till late evening, which explained why she couldn't ride during the day. The fine horse she was sitting on was called Peace and the man, Walter, was his owner. And what was most important, they arranged to meet again the following night.

I kept coming back every night and most of the times she was there, riding. I thought she rode really well, but Walter, who turned out to be a professional dressage trainer, saw it differently and corrected her a lot. He was quite hard on her. Silvia took it well, though, and did her best to follow his commands. Walter's training methods apparently worked for even I could tell she was improving. During the two months I had been watching them she had made huge progress, and I was sure that one day she was going to be an excellent dressage rider.

I envied her. She had her whole life ahead of her and could do what she really liked. For Silvia, the United States of America was truly a land of unlimited opportunities. But not for me anymore! I hadn't seen sunlight in more than thirty years. I became a creature of the night and the only one I had left was my Irish Wolfhound mix Ricky. Well, and Alex of course, who was actually responsible for the whole situation.

Once I was happy, too. I was twenty-five, had a beautiful wife and a nice house on the outskirts of Santa Rosa, in the heart of Sonoma Wine Country. Together with my best friend Zac, we ran a small construction company and on weekends I played baseball for the local amateur team Santa Rosa Rose Buds. Business was flourishing, my wife Linda and I were trying to have a baby and I couldn't wait to be a father. I thought life couldn't get much better than that.

The first blow came when I found out Linda had been cheating on me with Zac. Once I came home early from training and caught them together in our bed. I was devastated. She was my first big love and I thought we would grow old together. I was so desperate that I tried to save our marriage, but Linda said it was over and moved to Zac's. I lost my wife and my "best friend" on the same day, and as I couldn't work with Zac anymore, I decided to sell my half of the company. I got a good price for it but instead of enjoying the money, I turned to drinking.

Several weeks later, the second blow came. It was a warm summer night and I was returning home from my favorite brewery in Calistoga. I was drunk but not so much that it stopped me from driving. My reflexes were still quite good, and I would have probably made it home fine if I hadn't run into Alex (literally). It happened shortly after I passed the Petrified Forest, which was named after its petrified, over three-million-year-old redwood trees. We used to hike there with Linda and Ricky, and every time I drove by it, I felt a great grief for my lost life. I drove slowly, immersed in my sad thoughts, unaware of Alex speeding towards me down the side road. He was testing his new 1982 Pontiac Firebird, not expecting to meet anyone in the woods at that hour. So when I suddenly emerged in front of him from behind a tree, he had no chance to stop, and hit me from the right. The impact threw my van into the crash barrier on the opposite side of the road and the last thing I remember was how I smashed my head against the side window.

What happened next, I know only from Alex's narration. He got out of his mangled new toy, removed the broken glass from my driver's door and examined my unconscious body. As my skull was cracked open and I was bleeding badly, it was more than obvious I wasn't going to make it. I am not sure why (maybe he had a twinge of conscience for killing an innocent or he just decided he had been alone for too long), but he didn't leave me there to die. Instead, he sank his fangs into my wrist and drained me of blood to the point of death. Then he cut his own wrist and let his blood drip into my mouth.

When I came to myself again, something was wrong. I was still stuck in the driver's seat of the steaming wreck of my van but I was totally unharmed. My hands were deathly pale and my throat was burning with terrible thirst. My relief that I had survived the accident was soon replaced by true horror when Alex told me what I had become. He turned me into a vampire!

I checked my wrist and there was no pulse. I put my hand on my heart but it wasn't beating.

"What have you done to me?!" I cried out in desperation.

"Get out of the car!" Alex commanded, ignoring my emotional outburst.

I obeyed and jumped out of the wreck with unexpected ease and grace.

While I was examining my perfect body, Alex explained to me dryly what had to be done. "We need to hide both vehicles in the woods and remove all identification signs from them. Then we will feed you."

I will never forget my first hunt. I was suddenly so strong and fast that my prey had no chance. It was a deer. I brought it down to the ground after only a few strides and pierced the tough skin on its neck with my sharp fangs as if it was butter. The taste of blood was fantastic! I had never had anything so good in my life! I sucked the animal's blood insatiably, feeling its strength entering my body and filling every part of it with life. When I finished and the deer was dead, I wanted more, but Alex wouldn't let me kill another one.

"That's enough! You must learn to control your thirst."

So I tried, and the first two nights I did quite well, but then came the night I went to get Ricky. Linda and I had taken him from a shelter four years ago and I simply couldn't leave him locked in my house to starve to death. Because Alex had no idea I had an animal, he just thought that I went to get my stuff. Even though he worried I might do something stupid, I managed to persuade him to let me go alone. I told him it would look suspicious if anyone saw him at my house at night.

My plan was to load Ricky into Alex's second car, a navy Ford Bronco, take him to Zac's and drop him off in his backyard with a note for Linda asking her to take good care of him (she owed me at least that). As my parents lived in Idaho, she was the only one I could turn to. Now I know I should have dropped my house keys in Zac's mailbox with the message for Linda to pick Ricky up herself but, honestly, I'm glad I didn't.

At first everything went smoothly. I parked at the back of my house, slipped inside through the kitchen door and found Ricky on the floor next to an empty bowl. He looked confused and frightened but otherwise all right. He lay still staring at me for a while, as if trying to figure out what had happened with his sometimes drunk but otherwise quite normal human, and then the chase began. It was a very short one, though. The old boy being already nine and weakened by the lack of food, I had him inside one of Alex's sacks for dead deer before he knew it. I put him in the trunk and hit the road.

Fifteen minutes later, I pulled over in a dark spot near Zac's house. I got the note for Linda ready and went to the trunk to get the sack, but when I picked it up, Ricky started to bark inside like crazy. Realizing he was going to wake up the whole neighborhood and give me away, I had to do something. It was my first critical situation as a vampire, and I dealt with it the best I could. I opened the sack and bit poor Ricky on his neck.

While I was drinking his blood, I started to think straight again and realized what I was doing. *Oh no! I am killing my own dog!* I stopped abruptly and examined Ricky. He was quiet and still, as if he was dead, but I could tell he was still breathing. Suddenly, I knew what I had to do, and without thinking it through I did the same thing Alex had done to me two nights earlier – I cut my wrist and let my blood drip into Ricky's mouth. Not waiting to see what effect it would have on him, I closed the trunk and drove off.

It didn't take long, and loud bumping noises started to come from the back of the car. *He is hungry!* I drove slowly thinking about what to do while praying not to run across a police patrol car. I didn't come up with much, though, and the closer I was getting to Alex's cottage in the woods near Lake Sonoma, the more nervous I was. I had no idea whether changing an animal was forbidden or not, but I had a strong feeling it was wrong, and Alex would be mad at me. Although I didn't know him well yet, it was more than obvious he wasn't one to mess with.

Alex became a vampire in the late sixties when he was thirty-four. He was a professional gambler and one of the top cheats in Las Vegas. Being excellent at mathematics, he was almost invincible in counting cards, and as he had really nimble fingers, there weren't many who could swindle with chips like him. He kept his wins moderate, and never stayed in one casino for too long, so he was never caught. He made quite a good living out of it.

And it was his talent that cost him his mortal life. A vampire noticed what he was doing and started to follow him around. When he was certain it was more than good luck, he realized how useful it would be to have him for a companion (even vampires needed money to exist in the modern world). One night he waited for Alex in front of a casino and changed him in a dark alley. A few minutes later Alex killed his first human.

He played the role of the goose that laid golden eggs patiently for several months, but when he had learned everything he needed to survive in his new world, he set his maker on fire and watched him burn like a torch. Alex never forgets.

After that, he traveled round the States alone. During the years, he came across several vampires but as they kept asking about his maker, he tried to avoid them. According to vampire laws, killing one's maker is one of the most severe crimes, right after changing a child or an animal.

Alex evaded other vampires for one more reason. He was scared that if they found out he had an unlimited source of blood, they would want it for themselves. With the help of some local crooks, he set up several blood banks in South America and became totally independent of killing humans or animals. He knew that with modern medicine and police investigative methods, he just couldn't go on killing people without getting caught for much longer, and considering the diminishing game population, it was the only solution.

He paid his human servants generously, and they would never even think about deceiving him because they knew who they were dealing with. The poor blood donors believed their blood went to private hospitals. And some of it really did, but it was just a cover. At least they got paid quite well considering local conditions. This only went to show that some things will never change – if you have enough money, there is almost nothing you can't buy.

No matter how slowly I drove, I eventually reached Alex's cottage and had to face the consequences of my actions.

Alex was absolutely furious. "Have you lost your mind?! Changing an animal is strictly forbidden!!! We must destroy it!"

"No, Alex, please!" I pleaded. "Give him a chance! He has always been a great dog. I will train him, I promise! Take it as a chance to redeem what you did to me."

I managed to gain some time but as I didn't trust Alex, I stayed alert for many nights, never leaving Ricky alone with him.

Ricky didn't take his change very well, so the beginnings were hard. I fed him blood several times a night, yet he was still too mad to work with. Keeping him safe from Alex wasn't easy either. Almost every night, he claimed we had already given the dog his chance and that it was time to end it. But I didn't give up, and as the weeks passed, Ricky slowly started to calm down.

About a month after I changed him, when he finally seemed to be his old self again, I took him hunting for the first time. It didn't go too well, and before I realized what he was up to, he was tracking a group of humans who were hunting several miles from us. Luckily I managed to catch him before he reached them, and since Alex didn't know about it, it wasn't such a disaster after all.

I got Ricky a leash, something I had never needed for him before, and started to train him. Within less than three months, I turned him into the best hunting dog one could have ever wished for. He was practically invisible and quiet as a ghost, but when I gave him the cue to strike, he was faster than a bullet. He went straight for the artery on the neck, pierced it with a single bite, and drained the pray of blood without spilling a single drop. I had never seen a cleaner killer. Alex was quite impressed.

A faint noise reached our sensitive ears from the Bells' house and both Ricky and I turned our heads in that direction. It was shortly after ten and the Bells were still up watching TV.

Peter's silhouette appeared behind the sliding glass door.

"Sometimes I wonder what she is doing up there all those nights," Amanda's voice remarked from the living room.

"Riding?" Peter answered, watching as Silvia's head appeared in regular intervals in the closest corner of the arena. They had just started to canter.

"Are you sure they're just riding?" Amanda asked skeptically.

"Amanda! He could be her father!" Peter exclaimed, sounding shocked.

"And....? Some girls like older men," she kept pressing her point.

"Silvia isn't like that." Peter objected. "I spoke with Walter the other day and he said she was really talented. He wants to teach her as much as he can while she's here."

"Of course, he does," Amanda agreed, smiling to herself.

They continued watching TV in silence for a while, and then went to bed. A few moments later, I heard them breathing in their sleep.

I was really pissed off at Amanda. How could she say things like that about Silvia?! *She wouldn't sleep so well if she knew what I could do to her!* I thought. But like Silvia and Walter, the Bells had no idea I was watching them at night and it had to stay that way.

I almost gave myself away once, though. It happened only a few days after I started watching Silvia. Peace smelled me when I came too close to the arena, and he stood up on his hind legs. I was sure Silvia was going to fall. Thank God she stayed in the saddle, and after I retreated to my safe spot, they managed to calm Peace down.

They thought it had been a mountain lion. They couldn't have known it didn't come to our side of the mountain anymore, like the deer that had left to find a new home the night we moved in. They could be at peace, though. Their herd was small and we didn't want to attract attention by illegal hunting. And the one mountain lion? We left it alone. He was a survivor like us.

The lack of hunting opportunities was one of the reasons why Alex didn't like it on Mt. Diablo. Although he found my obsession with Silvia silly, especially when I didn't intend to kill her, I at least had some distraction on the mountain. But there was nothing for Alex, and without his computer, he would have been bored to death.

What we both missed equally, though, was the city. All the lights and beautiful views made us feel almost alive again. Moreover, the Castro was the right neighborhood for creatures like us. Two men walking a dog in the middle of the night – perfectly normal there. I liked our apartment on Market Street. With the small underground adjustments we had made, it felt like a real home. Our landlord must have been surprised when he lifted the living room carpet and found the trapdoor to our crypt. We had been renting the place for two years and would have stayed longer if we hadn't run into Hakan.

We met him in an Indian casino east of Sacramento a few days before the New Year. Although with the invention of the Internet, we started making money mainly by playing poker online, yet still went to casinos occasionally just for the fun of it. Hakan was the first vampire I had met after Alex, and I sensed his presence long before he joined our table. He was an old vampire with a young Indian face, quite friendly but too nosy. We answered his questions as vaguely as possible, aware that we had much to hide.

Hakan started to play with us but he had no chance. Alex, who was pretty good by himself, became absolutely unbeatable with my little help. Our signals were totally inconspicuous and we were never accused of collusion. When we hit Vegas every six years or so, we split up and each of us gambled in a different casino. I learned quite a lot from my maker, so we won even more this way. Surprisingly, we never got into any big trouble. The trick is to know when to leave. Unless you take a huge sum of money from the casinos, they don't really pay any attention to you. They even like occasional big winners because they encourage other players to bet more.

Hakan lost all his money after only a few games and furiously stormed out of the casino. We thought we wouldn't see him again, but he reappeared from thin air while we were getting into our van two hours later, claiming that half of what we had just won belonged to him.

"You picked the wrong casino! You shouldn't have cheated in my territory!" he threatened, his friendliness gone.

Alex would have rather started a nasty fight than share his money, but despite not liking it either, I had to stop him. With Ricky in the motel room only five miles away, we couldn't afford to risk him following us. So I gave the vampire what he wanted and he left peacefully with a satisfied grin on his face.

Alex didn't believe though, that Hakan was going to leave us alone so easily, and after the incident, he didn't feel safe in the Castro anymore.

"We have to move again," he said only a few nights later.

"Why?" I didn't understand. "Hakan will never find us in San Francisco!"

But Alex didn't share my optimism. "He is an old vampire with special powers. With the information we gave him, it won't be hard for him to trace us here."

I found Alex quite paranoid then, but I guessed that was why he was still around.

He didn't want to go to the cottage by the lake either. It was our last sanctuary, and if Hakan traced us there, we would have nowhere to go. So we started to look for a new home. It was me who found the old cottage on the slope of Mount Diablo. It was sufficiently remote, apart from other houses and it was for rent – a perfect hideaway for a few months.

Silvia was almost done riding for the night, only walking Peace, whose head was so low that his nose was almost touching the ground, in big circles. It was my favorite part because she talked with Walter about other things than riding and I usually learned something new about her. But that night I couldn't stay as Alex and I were picking up another delivery of blood near Livermore.

The carrier boxes with the blood bags usually arrived in a cooling truck with frozen vegetables, this way it didn't give the blood a bad smell like fish, and we transferred them to our built-in cooler hidden under the tailgate floor. With Ricky on it, no one ever dared to examine it closely.

I left our hiding place and set off for the cottage with much less enthusiasm than Ricky. I wasn't sure how many more nights "with Silvia" I had because Alex, who didn't like how everything around was getting drier and drier, had already started looking for a new place up north. The cottage was surrounded by oak trees from three sides, so if a fire broke out, it would burn down in no time. We would probably be fine in our tombs in the stone cellar, but it would be the end of us anyway if the firemen found us there during the day.

If it were up to me, I would have taken the risk and stayed on the mountain close to Silvia, but what difference would it make? There was no future for us. I couldn't approach her without telling her who I was, and she was returning home in a few months anyway. Back to Romania where it all started...

6

HORSE SHOW

Summer vacation started and with no school, I watched the boys the whole day. I suddenly realized what else I liked about my English classes so much – it was my precious time off. Without it, making it through my working day required much more effort and patience. Being stuck on the mountain the whole day didn't help either. There wasn't much to do, and when the boys got bored, which was often, they fought and argued, giving me a hard time. There were days when I had to drive them to Clayton so I wouldn't go nuts.

I wanted to start taking them to Theresa's again, but with Mack there, it wasn't a very good idea. The boys liked to come close to his stall, and I had to watch them carefully so they wouldn't get hurt. Because I got hardly any work done, I gave up after a couple of visits, deciding it wasn't worth the risk.

Fortunately, 4th of July was coming soon and the boys had something to look forward to. As it turned out, it was one of my best days of that summer, too.

In the morning, I went with the Bells to downtown Clayton to watch the parade. The whole town was there including the town council, the Clayton fire fighters, and the police department. It was quite a spectacle – polished classic cars, cowboys and Mexican vaqueros on beautiful horses, and an endless kiddie parade with kids on decorated bicycles, scooters, and other vehicles. Patriotic music was playing, and stars and stripes were everywhere you looked. I had never seen people so proud of their country.

After the parade I returned home with the Bells. Since it was a holiday and I didn't have to watch the boys, I changed into my riding clothes and hurried to Theresa's for my first daylight training with Walter. Although I rode in the morning on weekends, it was always on my own because Walter was busy training his other students.

I enjoyed the lesson a lot. We had been working on collection for weeks and it seemed I was finally getting the hang of it.

"Everything is in the outside rein! Outside rein and inside leg!" Walter shouted at me for the hundredth time.

And then, after many circles in trot, several figure-eights and a few half halts, Peace's head came down and I could feel the energy building below me. *I did it, I got him on the bit!* I didn't really understand everything Walter had been trying to explain to me about impulsion, engagement and the flow of energy, but I suddenly felt it was all there.

"Now try to extend his strides," Walter invited me after letting me do several circles in a collected trot.

„Open your thighs, move your legs slightly forward and let the energy flow!"

I tried to do as he said but nothing happened.

"Think forward!" he advised.

How on Earth can anyone think forward?! I was quite skeptical, but I tried it again. And all of a sudden it happened. I was being carried on Peace's long strides like on rolling waves. *Holy cow!* It was a wonderful feeling.

"Good! Good!" Walter praised me maybe for the third time in two months. It was then that I realized everything he was teaching me was some kind of philosophy, and to be able to ride according to it, I had to engage not only every part of my body, but also my mind.

Naturally, I was in high spirits for the rest of the day and the upcoming event only added to my good mood. Later in the afternoon, Walter was taking Theresa and me to the 4 of July barbecue at the horse club where he trained. Although I had no time to prepare any food, we were all set as Theresa loaded Walter's trunk with enough goodies to feed at least a dozen people. We drove towards Clayton, but just before we got there, Walter turned left onto a narrow road which led up the mountain. A few minutes later, we were entering Mt. Diablo Trail Ride Association.

The parking lot was almost full but Walter found a space by a stable with paddocks, and Theresa filled our hands with trays of food. She herself seized a big bowl of salad and we followed Walter to the clubhouse by the pool where everyone was gathered. The atmosphere inside was friendly and homey, and it reminded me of the New Year's Eve party at the horse place in Walnut Creek. The only difference was that there weren't any cowboy hats there because everyone rode English.

We helped ourselves to some food and chatted with Walter's friends for a while, and later Walter showed us around. There were two riding arenas, a dressage court and a cross country jump course. With direct access to acres and acres of trails, it was a great horse facility.

"It's a shame you can't keep Peace and Mack here." I sighed, despite knowing Walter couldn't afford to pay the stabling they asked for.

"Yeah, Mack would really love the trails – well, if I found someone brave enough to ride him," Walter said.

"Peace doesn't like trailing?" I asked with surprise.

"Well, he probably wouldn't complain, but it's not his favorite discipline. And as you know, with his delicate thoroughbred legs he is quite prone to injuries, so you'd have to avoid really rocky trails."

I had to agree that Peace wasn't a typical trail horse.

Walter showed us the horses he was training, and then we returned back to the clubhouse. Not for long though, since as soon as the night fell, Walter grabbed three glasses and a bottle of sparkling wine, and led us back to his car.

"Where are we going?" I asked Theresa curiously.

But she just smiled and handed me the glasses to hold.

We drove through pitch black darkness up a winding road towards the summit till Walter pulled up at some view point. From there, we had the whole of Clayton below us and we could also see the lights of Concord behind it.

"It's beautiful" I praised the view.

Walter opened the wine and filled our glasses, but when I wanted to take a sip, he told me to wait. *For what?* But before long, my question was answered as the 4 of July fireworks erupted into the sky above Concord, turning the sight into something magnificent. We toasted us and the horses, and then enjoyed the show in silence while sipping the wine. It was a perfect ending to a perfect day.

But the main surprise was still to come. When the last sparkle died out and the sky turned black again, Walter turned to me and said, "Silvia, I've been thinking about the progress you've made, and decided to sign you up for a horse show."

I was totally taken aback. "What? Walter, I can't be in a horse show! I've only just started to learn to ride properly!" *He must be joking! I'd be the worst rider of all.*

"It's only a simple schooling show," Walter tried to calm me down.

"You just walk, trot and canter, and change directions when asked to. You already know all that!" And before I could protest he added, "The one I want to put you in is in three weeks, so we still have plenty of time to practice."

"In only three weeks?!" I exclaimed, alarmed.

"Don't worry, you'll enjoy it. It'll be fun!"

I wasn't so sure about that but didn't argue any further.

What the hell! Maybe it's a good thing. I mean, how many girls from Romania can say they have been in a horse show in California? And Peace will be there with me, so I don't need to worry.

If we had trained hard before July 4, it was nothing compared to our training before the show. We were working on transitions (my main weakness was walk to canter), the right tempo, and on keeping the same rhythm in particular gaits. On top of that, Walter started explaining lateral dressage movements to me. We began with an exercise called shoulder-in where the rider is supposed to bend the horse towards the center of the ring while making him go sideways. It was the most difficult thing Walter had taught me so far, and I was really glad it wasn't going to be in the show.

On the second Saturday in July, I even had two training sessions. After I had already ridden alone in the morning, Walter called me to say one of his students had cancelled and he was free for the rest of the day.

"Get Peace ready," he instructed me. "I'll be at Theresa's in an hour."

"But, Walter, I've already ridden today!" I objected.

"Doesn't matter, a bit of extra work won't hurt you or Peace. Go and get him ready. I want to try something."

Knowing that when Walter took something into his head, nothing could stop him, I went obediently to get Peace, who was running loose in the arena. But as soon as he spotted me with the saddle in my hands, he ran away from me and hid in his stall, which was something he had never done before. If he knew how, he would have closed the door behind him, too. I felt sorry for him, but I knew Walter wasn't going to call off the training, so I entered the stall prepared for a struggle. There was none, though, and Peace stood calmly as always, letting me saddle him up for the second time that day.

When Walter arrived almost two hours later (I had already gotten used to the fact that punctuality wasn't his strong side), he placed cavalletti and small jumps all over the arena. He claimed it was good for adjusting the stride length and also to improve Peace's balance. What followed was the toughest training I had ever had, and I wondered why Peace didn't throw me off his back.

In the middle of July, I celebrated my birthday. It fell on a Sunday that year and to my big surprise the Bells threw a birthday party for me with cake and everything. They even invited Walter and Theresa. We spent a very nice afternoon together and I got some great presents. The Bells gave me a beautiful leather-covered photo album for my pictures, Theresa presented me with a pair of amazing riding gloves and from Walter, I got the best book that had ever been written about dressage.

I turned twenty-three and everyone but the boys teased me about my age. Luckily, it didn't take long and the conversation turned to the Bells' upcoming trip to Europe. The boys were really excited about it, and they were telling Theresa about all the places they were going to visit. I found it rather strange that they would be in Europe while I stayed in California. It was almost as if we exchanged our lives. But I wasn't sorry I wasn't going with them – I was exactly where I wanted to be.

"When are you leaving?" Theresa asked Amanda.

"On July 30, early morning," she answered and gave her the details of their travel itinerary. "We land in Paris in the evening, have two days to explore the city and on August 2, we fly to Prague for the wedding. We're going to rent a car there to get around, and before we fly back from Vienna, Andrea wants to show us quite a few places in the Czech Republic. We'll be back on August 11."

"It's not fair," Theresa complained. "You'll see all those exciting places in Europe while I am just going to Oregon!"

"You'll be away as well?" Amanda asked, sounding surprised.

That was news for me, too, as Theresa hadn't mentioned anything.

"I'm going to visit my sister in Salem," she explained. "I'm leaving right after the horse show and will be gone for three weeks."

"Hmm, we'll have to find someone to take care of the goats then," Amanda said thoughtfully. "Silvia is taking her two weeks off, and we were kind of hoping you could feed them while we are in Europe."

"Don't worry about it, Amanda, I'll take care of them," I offered.

"Didn't you want to travel?" Peter looked surprised.

"Well, I decided to stay here," I replied uncertainly, knowing he wouldn't understand.

"But what about all the places you wanted to visit?" Peter objected. "It would be a shame if you returned to Romania seeing just New York and San Francisco."

"I'll have plenty of time for traveling during my thirteenth month," I said to assure him that wasn't going to happen. But the truth was that I didn't have any plans for my last month in the States either. The only thing I really wanted was to stay on Mt. Diablo and ride Peace for as long as I could.

After all, my decision to spend my vacation on the mountain worked best for everyone. Amanda and Peter were glad the house wouldn't stay empty and the goats would be fed, and Theresa was happy that I would take care of the horses and the ponies.

The following Sunday, Walter took me shopping for the last thing I didn't have for the horse show – a riding jacket. Or any jacket that resembled it. We were lucky and found what we were looking for in the first second hand store we entered.

It was a black jacket from nice material and it was for a great price. I tried it on and it fit perfectly. The length was right, too.

"That'll do," Walter said and pulled out his wallet.

"Walter, I can afford to buy a jacket for twenty dollars," I protested.

But he was already giving money to the cashier.

After the fastest shopping in my life, Walter decided to take me for dinner to a Mexican restaurant. He was a real gentleman, and I suddenly realized he was quite charming when he wasn't commanding me in the arena.

"How come you never got married?" I asked him out of curiosity as we were finishing our burritos.

Walter looked quite taken aback by my question, and I quickly apologized. "Sorry, I didn't mean to be nosy, it's none of my business."

"No, no, it's okay," he said. "I was married once, many years ago."

"Really?! What happened?" It came out before I could stop myself.

"You know, many things. It simply didn't work out. Maybe I just spent too much time around horses."

"She didn't like horses?" I asked.

"Of course, she did. Where do you think I met her?"

"In fact, Susan was a lot like you," he went on. "A natural talent. But she soon realized she wanted more from life than to ride seven days a week. After we divorced, she married a lawyer. They have two daughters and live in a big house in San Francisco. I think she is happy now."

Wow, she had a husband who shared her passion for horses, who encouraged and guided her in riding, and she exchanged him for a lawyer and a big house! She definitely wasn't like me! We sat in silence for a while till I spoke just to say something.

"What should I do with my hair for the show?"

"Hairnet!" Walter exclaimed.

"What?!" I asked.

"We need to buy you a hairnet," he explained and called the waiter.

Several minutes later, we hit the nearest drugstore and I got myself that strange accessory I would have never dreamed of wearing.

On Monday before the show, Walter came to our training with small metallic things in his hand. He went straight to my riding boots and started to put one on. They were spurs!

"No, no, no! I am not wearing those!" I protested. I had always connected spurs with ruthless riders who hurt horses.

But Walter ignored me and placed the second spur on my other boot.

"Here!" He handed them to me. "You should try them first before you decide. Your legs are so steady now that you will barely touch Peace with them. will look god in the show."

It was always so hard to oppose him. After all, Walter was right, I could at least try it. And then I remembered that Mike and Anthony wore them too, and they were definitely not ruthless riders.

I climbed on Peace carefully and spurred him gently into a walk. I was quite stiff at first, but after a few minutes, I forgot I had the spurs on and rode as normal. It was exactly as Walter said it would be – I barely touched Peace with them and I wasn't hurting him at all.

During the following four days, I got used to my new riding aid so well that I had no reason to argue about wearing it in the horse show. I had other things to do that morning anyway. First of all, I had to groom Peace perfectly and braid his main in little knots. Doing it for the first time in my life, I wasn't very good at it, so I was grateful for Walter's help. We did a great job and Walter also braided the top of Peace's tail. When we were done, Peace looked exquisite.

"Look at him, isn't he gorgeous?" Walter asked. "And it's only thanks to you."

"Thanks to me?" I repeated doubtfully.

But then Walter pointed at his well-defined muscles and I had to admit he didn't look like that when I started to ride him.

I stroked Peace's beautiful neck and then went inside Theresa's house to get myself ready. I cleaned up, brushed my hair and put on my white shirt and white leggings, which with some imagination resembled riding breeches. Theresa helped me tie the white riding stock Walter gave me and secured it with her beautiful antique brooch.

"It will bring you good luck."

"Thank you, Theresa," I said to her, my voice sounding strange. I suddenly realized I was getting quite nervous.

In less than two hours, I will be performing in a horse show! But what if it's a disaster? Walter put all his trust in me, what will he say if I fail him?! I panicked internally while Theresa styled my hair into a low bun and put the black hairnet on it.

But when we went outside and I saw Peace again, all my doubts were gone. We wrapped his feet in new white bandages that matched the saddle pad, and Walter led him to the horse trailer he had borrowed from the riding club. From all the preparations, Peace knew he was going to some kind of competition and remembering his job well, he climbed in gracefully without a trace of hesitation.

Who had a problem with that, though, was Mack. His favorite human was leaving with Peace and wasn't taking him with them – that was intolerable! I had never seen a horse rampage like that. I thought he would either hurt himself or break the rails. Walter tried to calm him down, but with no results.

"He will calm down once we're gone," he ensured us as we were getting into the car.

Although it was hard to believe, I had no time to worry about Mack as I had to focus on the last instructions Walter was giving me on the way to the show.

"And you should be prepared that Peace will be different when we get there," he warned me. "You know, unfamiliar place, strange horses, a lot of people… Forget about the sweet Peace you know. He'll be quite anxious."

Great! I am nervous already and Peace will be nervous too! This can't end well! I started to panic again.

"Don't worry, you'll handle him," Walter added fast when he saw my expression. "Just get him on the bit and you should be fine."

I took several deep breaths and decided not to think about it.

When we arrived at Heather Farm in Walnut Creek, most of the riders were already in the saddle. I put on my "riding" jacket and looked around to assess my competition.

"Walter, look at that black horse over there!" I remarked with admiration. "His nose is perfectly vertical. And how beautifully his neck is arched! I've never managed to collect Peace like that."

"It's a headset," Walter said coldly.

"What is it?" I asked, not familiar with the term.

"It's artificial. They ride the horse with side reins attached to the saddle for so long that he gets used to it and carries his head like that no matter what. Look at his hollow back – it's not a real collection."

"Oh," I breathed out, feeling pity for the horse.

We saddled Peace up together and then we separated. Walter went to sign us in and pay the registration fee, while Theresa accompanied me and Peace to the warm-up ring where training was in full swing.

Not paying attention to the other riders, as I wouldn't be able to evaluate them anyway, I started to walk Peace in big circles to let him get used to his new surroundings. Walter was wrong for the first time I had known him. Peace was as sweet as always! Well, a bit forward, but that was in fact very pleasant. I managed to bring his head down after only a few circles of trot and Theresa gave me a thumbs-up. So far, it was going more than well.

But the show was about to begin and we were asked to enter the show ring before I'd had a chance to bring Peace to canter. *Damn it, Walter, we should have come earlier!* I sighed while checking the parking lot for the last time. Suddenly, my annoyance was replaced by joy as I saw Peter, Amanda and the boys getting out of their minivan. *They made it!* Although they had promised they would come, I wasn't giving it much of a chance. Neither Peter nor Amanda were big horse fans, so I thought they might forget or have better plans.

During the show I ignored everything around me, and focused only on riding. There was just Peace, me and the voice from the speaker. I even had no idea Peter was recording it. The instructions were clear and simple, and I followed them without any problems. I found it quite easy. Peace was great and when I brought him to canter, it was absolutely fantastic. He was like a well-tuned machine working at the highest performance level and I was enjoying myself so much that I almost wished the show lasted longer. But it was over soon and we were asked to line up in the middle of the arena. Knowing they would also judge the way the horses stood, I made sure I halted exactly how Walter taught me to.

We stood in the middle, having four horses on each side, and waited for the judges' verdict. Then they called the first name, and the girl next to me stepped out from the line and went to get her ribbon for first place. What followed was the biggest surprise of my life.

"Silvia Milescu on horse Dash for Peace and Freedom," I heard my name pronounced with an American accent. I couldn't believe it – we were second!

I gave Peace a cue and we walked for our first ribbon.

They evaluated the horses next, and this time I wasn't as surprised to hear Peace's full name again because they would have had to be blind not to see he was a great horse. He came first!

When I joined my small fan club, I was overwhelmed with emotion. I didn't dream of such a success.

"Congratulations!" Theresa hugged me and whispered to my ear, "I knew it!"

Peter and Amanda were quite impressed by my riding and the boys were even more excited from the ribbons than I was. The only one who was disappointed was Walter.

"You should've been first!" he grumbled. "You rode better than the girl who won."

But even if that had been true (which I honestly doubted), I wouldn't have minded at all. Second place was much more than what I had hoped for, and I finally realized that, although I was too tall to become a jockey, I could still achieve something in the equestrian world.

Suddenly, I couldn't imagine returning back to Romania in only two months and abandoning everything. *I can't leave! Not now, when I've found the horse of my life and the best trainer I will ever have.*

7

Bad Idea

It was another hot day on Mt. Diablo and Steve was over at David's place. They were best friends and, apart from their family vacations, spent their summer breaks together. Both were seventeen and lived on Morgan Territory Road.

"What'll we do now?" Steve asked David when he got tired of playing games on his X-box.

David suddenly got an idea. "We can have a beer or two. My dad won't notice if some are missing."

"Cool!" Steve agreed.

They went to the garage and David took a pack of four Heinekens from their second fridge, but as they were returning back to David's room, they heard a noise coming from the front door.

"Mom!" David whispered.

They turned around and hurried back to the garage. David hid the beers in the trunk of his Ford Mondeo, his mom's old car which he got for his sixteenth birthday, then grabbed two popsicles from the freezer and handed one to Steve.

"Hi mom, you're home early," David greeted Mrs. Anderson when they found her putting away groceries in the kitchen.

"Hi, boys! I'm glad to see you too, Dave! How was your day?" She never forgot to ask even if she already knew the answer.

"Fine," David replied as always and asked his standard question, "What's for dinner?"

They had lasagna and Mrs. Anderson invited Steve to have some with them.

After dinner David suggested that he would take Steve home, but his mom saw it differently.

"It's gonna be dark soon, I'll drive him myself," she said firmly.

"Mom, it's just a couple of miles! It's not like I was driving to San Francisco! Steve wants to show me some of his new CDs," David pleaded.

Mrs. Anderson sighed and exchanged a resigned look with her husband.

"All right, then, if it can't wait till tomorrow... but be back by nine!"

"Sure, mom!" David replied, and they were gone.

David drove slowly, wondering where to pull over.

When they were halfway to his house, Steve got an idea, "We can go to Theresa Marshall's place!"

His parents knew her well and Steve used to ride the old pony she'd had before Black Beauty.

"How'd you know she's not home?" David asked.

"We met her last week and she told my mom that she was leaving. She's visiting her sister in Oregon or something."

"Great, let's check it out," David agreed and after a few yards turned up Theresa's driveway.

The place looked deserted. There was no car in front of Theresa's house and the horses were closed in their stalls. David drove past the arena and parked on a patch of dirt behind the tuck shed where they couldn't be seen from anywhere. He turned off the engine and Steve got the beers from the trunk.

They drank slowly, savoring their beer while listening to Eminem and talking about their plans for their upcoming senior year in high school. Halfway through his second Heineken, David remembered the car battery wasn't in the best shape and started the engine. They chatted for another several minutes before deciding to get moving.

As they were leaving their hiding spot, the Ford's hot tailpipe brushed a small pile of hay on the ground by the arena entrance and a spark ignited the straw. A small fire broke out and soon after the car vanished around the bend of Theresa's driveway, flames spread to a bigger pile of hay that was piled against the wooden wall of the arena. It was August 2, 8:15 p.m., and the sun was just setting over the Pacific Ocean.

8

Fire

"Silvia, will you take us to the airport?" Peter asked me the day before their departure to Europe.

"Are you sure?" I said, taken aback by his request.

"Don't worry, your driving has improved considerably since you came here. I have no doubts you will manage the freeway fine," he replied.

But it wasn't just driving on the freeway that worried me. I was also concerned I would get lost on the way back from San Francisco. Although I took that route several times with the Bells, I didn't pay much attention to where we were going as I wasn't driving. Peter assured me though, that once I knew what signs to follow, it was quite easy.

"Okay then," I agreed, knowing that they would have to ask some friends of theirs from Clayton if I refused.

We set out at two in the morning. Peter was driving and I focused on the road more than ever, listening intently to his instructions for my drive back. When we arrived at the airport, Peter got their luggage from the trunk and after we exchanged our safe trip wishes, the Bells disappeared inside the airport terminal.

I climbed behind the wheel, took a deep breath and hit the road. There was almost no traffic and soon I was approaching the Bay Bridge, leaving San Francisco behind. I followed the signs like Peter had told me and before I knew it, I was getting off the freeway in Walnut Creek. *That was really easy!*

While I was driving through the deserted streets of Clayton, I realized how tired I was. It was still dark and I already pictured myself crawling back into my bed. My eyelids suddenly became so heavy that I had to focus hard on keeping my eyes open and didn't really see the black cat before it jumped in front of my car. I slammed on the breaks and swerved the steering wheel at the same time, avoiding the cat but hitting the right curb.

"Damn it!" I swore.

At least the cat made it to the other side of the road unharmed. I wasn't superstitious, nevertheless, I couldn't help recalling that in Romania a black cat crossing one's path was an omen of misfortune and death. I knew there was something I should do to break the curse, but I couldn't remember what it was. *Don't be silly, it's nonsense!* I shook my head and got out of the car to check the damage. Although the tire was okay, the plastic wheel cover was dented inwards. *Great! I'll have to fix it before the Bells return!*

In the afternoon, I drove back to Clayton to get some groceries, and I stopped at the garage. The mechanic examined the wheel cover closely, and then eyed me suspiciously. "You must've hit the curb real hard!"

Well, I already know that! I thought and asked him how much it would cost me to have it fixed, expecting a figure I wasn't going to like.

He said nothing and vanished inside the garage.

A moment later, he was back with a screwdriver in his hand. He placed it between the tire and the wheel cover and forced the plastic back to its original position. It already looked almost like before.

"Leave the car parked in the sun for a couple of days and it'll be as good as new," he said and returned back to the garage.

Problem solved for free! It seemed the black cat had brought me good luck after all.

With the Bells in Europe and Theresa in Oregon, I became the temporary mistress of two nice big houses and an arena. It wasn't a bad feeling at all! And a big responsibility too, which I was fully aware of. Watering plants and looking after the goats took me only a short while and since I had already been taking care of Peace, Mack and the ponies anyway, I suddenly had plenty of free time. I was planning to spend most of it with Peace, letting him out of his stall as much as possible to repay him a little for his hard work before the show, but what happened only three days after the Bells' departure thwarted all my plans.

I remember the last day of my human life like it was yesterday. It was a Friday and I woke up to another bright sunny morning on the mountain. I had my favorite breakfast (cereals and yogurt), got dressed into my riding clothes and hurried to Theresa's, the black cat long forgotten.

At 10 a.m., I had all the work done and was getting Peace ready for our morning training. Walter was late as usual and when he finally arrived, I was almost done riding. But he brought something – a portable stereo.

"Are you going to play some relaxing music to Mack?" I joked as Mack had been really grumpy lately. We couldn't blame him, though. Turning all his attention to my training, Walter had hardly any time for him in weeks. I couldn't even recall when he last longed him.

"No, it's not for Mack. The music is for you and Peace. You will ride to it," Walter explained.

What?! I thought he was joking, but he wasn't. He pressed PLAY on the CD player and some classical music started to come out of the speakers. It was Vivaldi and even I, who had always been quite ignorant to that kind of music, had to appreciate its beauty.

I asked Walter why classical music and he told me that dressage and classical music went together like peanut butter and jelly. I made peanut butter and jelly sandwiches for the boys, so I understood it was a great combination.

Having no idea how to ride to music, I simply started to trot. I didn't feel bad at all. The music was very light and cheerful and suited Peace's delicate movements. It was even better once I picked up the rhythm. Or at least I thought so, since Walter was correcting me all the time:

"A bit faster!"

"Slow down!"

"Keep the tempo!"

However, when the CD stopped playing, he said to my surprise, "That wasn't bad at all for a first try."

"It's a big shame you can't stay longer," he continued. "The three of us, we could've done big things together. You could've been winning dressage competitions in less than a year!"

I suddenly felt it was the right time to tell him about my decision. "Actually, I don't intend to return back to Romania in October. I want to stay here for another year and keep riding Peace."

"Of course, if that's okay with you," I added fast.

"Are you kidding?! Of course, I want you to stay! Peace has been waiting for you since I stopped riding him. It will break his heart when you leave. The longer you stay the better."

I let out a huge sigh of relief! I had been hoping for an answer like that.

"But where will you stay?" Walter wanted to know. "The Bells said that you were their last au-pair."

That was true. Since Christopher was starting school that fall, they didn't really need an au-pair anymore.

"I'll have to find a new host family. I called the agency on Monday, and they told me they could extend my au-pair visa for another year," I explained.

"And what if you don't find a family by October?" Walter asked.

That was one of the two weak points of my otherwise perfect plan. The families I knew already had an au-pair, and the closest host family listed at the agency lived in L.A., which would have been great, except I wanted to stay in Contra Costa County.

"I simply have to," I replied. "I'm going to put ads in local papers and on some public places. I'll also ask Amanda for help when she returns from Europe. She knows quite a few people, you know."

The Bells didn't know about my intention to stay yet. They were really busy before their departure to Europe and I didn't want to bother them with my problems.

"That sounds good! I'm sure you'll find someone. But if you don't, you can always stay in my house," Walter suggested.

Wow! He is a real friend.

"Thanks Walter, I really appreciate it," I said, despite knowing I wasn't going to accept his offer. I didn't want to be a burden to anyone.

My savings weren't big, and without a work visa, I would run out of money in only a few months. So, if I ruled out getting married – there was almost no chance of that, not that I would get married for a green card – finding a new host family was my only chance.

The other weak point of my plan was my mom. She looked forward to having me back so much that I worried it would break her heart if I told her I wasn't coming home. So I decided not to tell my parents anything until I was one hundred percent sure I was staying.

When Walter left, I went to the Bells' house for lunch, leaving Peace and the ponies in the arena. I made myself a sandwich and went on the computer to create the ad; once I had it approved by Walter, I didn't want to lose a single day. I wrote that I was an experienced au-pair and that I would be available in two months. At the end, I mentioned I was staying near Clayton, and that I would be more than happy to meet in person before they made a decision.

I printed out several copies to get started and went back to Theresa's to switch the horses – I put Mack in the arena and let the ponies run outside freely. I wanted to walk Peace on a lead rope to let him graze, but the grass around Theresa's place was so dry that he wasn't interested in it. So I climbed to the loft and threw down several armfuls of hay. While both Peace and Mack stood calmly by their heaps eating, Spirit and Black Beauty kept running about, spreading the hay all over the place.

At five I realized that if I wanted to go to the gym, I should get moving. I hadn't been there since I started riding Peace and it was high time to make use of my membership. I decided to leave cleaning up the hay for the morning, so I just closed everyone in their stalls and returned to the Bells' house. There I took a shower, dressed directly into my gym clothes, and after grabbing some food and the ad printouts, I set out for Clayton. I parked at the Safeway where I placed one ad on their message board, and walked to the Clayton Fitness Center that was just across the parking lot.

"You're still here! We haven't seen you for so long that we thought you'd already left!" A guy from the gym called Nick greeted me warmly.

I told him that I was actually looking for a new host family so that I could stay longer, and he willingly displayed my ad on their notice board by the entrance and even promised to ask around for me.

I had a great workout. It felt really good to stretch and to exercise the muscles I didn't use when riding. And maybe it was the released endorphins that caused me to suddenly feel quite optimistic about the future. *I won't have to leave! I'll find a new host family near Mt. Diablo, ride Peace at night and everything will stay as it has been till now.* I already pictured myself in dressage competitions. Perhaps I was aiming too high though, like Icarus who came so close to the Sun that his wings melted and he fell into the sea.

From the gym, I drove directly to Theresa's to feed the horses and to check everything before I went to bed. When I turned up Theresa's driveway and saw light coming through the oak trees, I thought at first that someone had turned the arena lights on. But the glow was too bright, way too bright for the arena lights! There was no doubt that it was a fire! I slammed on the gas and soon had a full view on the work of destruction – the whole left side of the arena was in flames. Fighting tears, I let out a jerky sigh of relief. I came in time. The stalls weren't burning yet!

I jumped out of the car and ran towards Peace's paddock. The air was hot and full of smoke, and the horses' desperate neighing was drowned out by the loud cracking of burning wood. Through the railing, I saw Peace shuffling around nervously in his stall. Next to him, Mack was kicking the rails with all his strength, determined to get out of that hell at any cost.

After struggling a bit to unlatch the gate that opened from inside, I ran through Peace's paddock and opened his stall. Peace had never been happier to see me. I led him out by his halter and sent him off towards Theresa's house. Then I ran back for Mack. The second I opened his stall, he sprang forward through his paddock like a racing horse. A moment later, I watched him galloping away down Theresa's driveway. Peace, who had been trotting around not sure where to go, followed him, and they both vanished in the dark. *Don't go further than to the old cottage! Please!* I prayed with the memory of the steep rocky trail behind it running through my head.

But there was no time to worry about them – I still had to get the ponies out. I faced the burning arena again, took a deep breath and ran inside through Mack's stall. The fire had already spread to the loft, and the ponies retreated to the railing on the opposite side of their stall, petrified by the approaching flames. I opened the gate but they wouldn't move – the fire was too close. I had no choice but to go for them and drag Black Beauty out by her halter. Luckily, Spirit followed right behind her.

As we were finally entering the arena, Black Beauty slipped out of my grip and both ponies ran outside through Mack's open stall. At that moment, I heard a loud cracking sound. I looked back and saw that the loft had detached from the arena wall and was falling right onto me. I shot forward in a desperate attempt to escape but managed to make only a few strides before something heavy knocked me down to the ground and everything went black.

The last ray of sun vanished in the Pacific Ocean and I instinctively opened my eyes. I rested uneasily that day, knowing it would be my last night on the mountain. It was a wonder we were still there. Alex had already bought a house in Seattle, and if I hadn't persuaded him to pick up another blood delivery before the journey, we would have been long gone. I reasoned that we should have a bigger reserve of blood in case something went wrong up north, but the truth was that I tried to postpone our departure because of Silvia. She hadn't showed up since the horse show though, and I started to worry that something had happened to her.

Aware it was my last chance to see her, I jumped out of my tomb, let Ricky out of his, and hurried upstairs to make us breakfast. I drank my daily share of blood almost as fast as Ricky and ran to the door. But when I reached for the door knob, I smelled something. I looked out of the window and saw two horses. They made a small circle in front of the cottage and then headed to the back. I recognized Peace and Mack immediately. *Walter's horses! Something must have happened!*

I ran back downstairs and told Alex, who was just getting up, what I had seen.

"Sorry, buddy!" I locked Ricky in the cellar and we went to find out what was going on.

The smell of smoke hit our noses the moment I opened the front door. There was a fire somewhere really close and the reddish glow above the oak trees told us where – Theresa's place! Suddenly, I had a horrible premonition. I ran as fast as I could, leaving Alex behind, and in a few moments I almost collided with Theresa's ponies as they were dashing away from the burning arena. I immediately spotted Silvia's red Honda, the driver's door wide open, parked in front of it. My worst fears came true – she was inside! I started towards the east sidewall, the only side of the arena that wasn't in flames yet.

"Have you lost your mind?! You will burn!" I heard Alex yelling after me.

Although I knew perfectly well what could happen, the only thing I was able to think of was that I had to save her. I jumped over the low wall of the ring and found Silvia's unconscious body inside. She was lying face-down in the sand, buried under burning remains of the loft. I ran to her and removed a heavy beam from her back. Then I took her hands and pulled her out of the debris. It wasn't a nice sight – her legs were badly burned, her sweatpants scorched to her skin. I carefully turned her on her back and put my arms under her shoulders and knees. She was still alive. I lifted her up and carried her across the ring back to the east wall, but before I got there, the arena roof started to collapse onto us with loud cracking noises. I sprang forward with all my might and we only narrowly escaped the falling beams.

"You made it!" Alex exclaimed with amusement when I joined him outside.

He was watering the grass in front of Theresa's house with her garden hose so that the fire wouldn't spread in our direction. He must have called the fire department, too, since the sound of sirens could be heard in the distance.

"Alex, take her car and park it in front of that house over there!" I pointed with my chin to the Bells' house. "They mustn't find out she was here."

"Brian, what the fuck d'you think you're doin'?! Leave her here! They'll take care of her. They'll give her skin from a pig or something. She'll be fine..." Alex was shouting after me, but I was already halfway to the cottage, knowing what had to be done.

Ricky looked really surprised when I appeared in the cellar with a human in my arms. Thinking I brought a second course, he approached us with a wagging tail and bared teeth.

"Stay!" I commanded and pointed to his place in the corner.

He gave me a hurt look, nevertheless turned around and started to walk there slowly.

I laid Silvia's unconscious body on the sofa and sat next to her. She looked so peaceful in her oblivion. For the moment, she wasn't suffering, but that was going to change soon. She was badly burned and would be in terrible pain for a really long time. I just couldn't let that happen. Even if it meant that she would hate me for the rest of her days for taking her life, I was willing to take the chance. Something deep inside was telling me that I was doing the right thing.

I took her delicate wrist in my hands, brought it to my mouth and sank my teeth into her soft skin. Then I started to drink her delicious blood – the blood I longed to taste since I first saw her.

David was on his way home from Steven's house with two CDs on the passenger seat as alibi. He drove slowly, knowing that after two beers his reflexes would be slower than usual. All of a sudden, he heard fire sirens and a few moments later, two fire trucks swept past him in the opposite direction. *Is there a fire somewhere?* he wondered. He pulled over and watched the trucks in the rear-view mirror. What was his surprise when they turned up Theresa's driveway.

"What the fuck?!"

He looked up the mountain and saw reddish-yellow flames blazing above the trees exactly where Theresa's place was. A feeling of pure horror struck him. He had no idea how, but he was almost certain that their presence at Theresa's place less than half an hour ago had something to do with this.

Despite suffering twinges of guilt for years, neither David nor Steve ever told anyone about their visit to Theresa's place. They knew they would have been in a really big trouble if they had, and so it stayed their secret forever. Their only consolation was that no one had died in the fire that night.

9

TRANSFORMED

When I came to myself again, I had no idea what day it was or where I was. It reminded me of the feeling I'd had when I first awoke in the Bells' house. I was lying on my back, and somehow I knew that it wasn't the position I was in when I had passed out. I felt different. There was no pain but my whole body was numb and my throat was burning with a terrible thirst. I had a strong gut feeling that something happened while I was out. Something important that changed everything.

I opened my eyes and found myself staring into an unfamiliar stone arched ceiling. I was in a cellar! I turned my head and met the intent blue gaze of a young man. He was tall and his handsome face was framed with brown wavy hair.

The young man smiled nervously and spoke, "How are you feeling?"

Am I hurt? I sat up, and the moment I saw my burned clothes, it all came back to me – the fire, the horses, the falling loft.

I looked back at the man. "Did you save me?"

"Kind of," he said evasively.

Of course, he saved me. Otherwise I would be dead now!

"Thanks, I'm really grateful to you!" I said awkwardly.

I looked around and my eyes rested on a big gray dog that was lying in the corner watching us sadly. Suddenly, I knew exactly where I was and whom I was talking to. I was in that spooky cottage up Theresa's driveway and he was one of the two guys who lived there.

Where are the horses?" I asked straight away.

"The last time I saw them, they were heading up the trail behind our house."

That was precisely what I had feared would happen!

"I must find them and bring them back," I said urgently.

"I'm sorry, but you can't go out now. The firemen must think you left before the fire."

"Why?! And how come I'm not burned?" *What's going on here?!*

He hesitated a little and then said gravely, "I changed you."

"You changed me?" I repeated and he nodded.

"Changed me into what?!" I asked, bewildered.

"I changed you into a vampire." He said it slowly, stressing the last word.

"A vampire, right!" I smiled skeptically. Well, I did feel different but how could he possibly turn me into a mythical creature that in fact didn't exist?

"Can you be serious now, please?!" I asked him, rising to my feet. "I don't have time for jokes, I really have to go!"

He stood up as well and smiled rather sadly. "There were times when I didn't believe in vampires either."

"You must be thirsty!" he added. "Stay here, I'll bring you something." And before I could protest, he was gone, locking the cellar door behind him.

"Damn it!" I swore. Although I had never been so thirsty in my entire life, I could endure it. The only thing I really needed was to get out of that damn cellar and find Peace.

Am I kept a prisoner? I thought, rejecting that idea immediately. He was no villain. *But why is he acting so strange? And why did he bring me down here?*

I decide to explore the room. To my right stood a coffee table with two laptops on it and two easy chairs. A big TV hung on the wall opposite the sofa where I had woken up a while ago. *Do they use the cellar as a living room?!* On my left, the cellar continued around the corner. I peeked in there and shivered. In the middle of the room, which was a bit smaller than the first one, were three open stone tombs. *The bedroom?!*

I collapsed back onto the sofa and looked down at my hands. In the dim light of the cellar, they seemed unnaturally pale as did the untouched skin on my legs, visible through the holes in my burned sweatpants. *What if he told me the truth? What if another secret world exists and I became a part of it?* I ran my tongue across my upper teeth and felt that my fangs were longer and sharper than I remembered them. It was scary how everything fit in his vampire theory. I didn't know what to believe anymore. It was like a bad dream you couldn't wake up from.

I suddenly realized I wasn't alone. The dog was still lying in the corner, not having moved an inch since his master had left. When I first met him, he scared me to death but that night he didn't look frightening at all. In fact, he was pretty cute.

"Come here!" I called him but he hesitated.

"Come here!" I called again and tapped on my thigh.

The dog got to his feet and started to walk slowly towards the sofa. When he came all the way to me, he sat at my feet and eyed me curiously.

"That's a good boy!" I praised him and stroked his head.

At that moment, the door opened and my rescuer was back with a big cup of some red liquid. A gorgeous scent filled the cellar. It smelled of vanilla, chocolate and berries, and of happiness, of hope, of my dreams, and secret desires. I suddenly couldn't concentrate on anything else.

"I see you've already made friends with Ricky," the man said interrupting my sensation. "By the way, I'm Brian."

"I'm Silvia," I said absentmindedly, not taking my eyes off the cup.

"I know," he remarked and passed it to me.

He knows my name? I was surprised but had no strength to ask questions. My whole world shrank into the content of that cup. I brought it to my lips and took a sip. It tasted divine. It was better than anything I had ever tried. Better than cookies and cream ice cream, better than pecan pie, better than the best wine. I took a long swig and felt the warmth spread through my entire body.

"Can I get more?" I asked automatically when the cup was empty.

Brian left once more and a few moments later returned with two more cups of that godly nectar. Only after I had finished it all, I started to think straight again and uncomfortable thoughts flooded my mind.

"What was it?" I asked fearfully.

Brian, who was just putting the last empty cup on the coffee table, turned to me and said matter-of-factly, "Blood."

Despite expecting that answer, it was still shocking to hear it.

I needed more information. "What blood?"

"Human blood."

Oh no! I had hoped it was animal. I ate animal meat and drinking its blood wouldn't have been such a difference. But feeding on something that belonged to a human?!

"Did you kill for it?" I asked in a small voice.

He smiled. "No, we don't do that. We have our donors."

I sighed with relief. *Thank God I am not responsible for someone's death!* Donors seemed okay, although I had no desire to know the details.

Brian sat down next to me on the sofa and we sat in silence for a while, immersed in our own thoughts. Well, at least he seemed to be since I couldn't think at all. His closeness was so unnerving! I peeked up at him several times and was suddenly fully aware of how tall and good- looking he was. Our eyes met once but we both quickly looked away.

What do you think you're doing?! I scolded myself silently. With everything I was going through, I couldn't have chosen a worse time to fall in love.

"Look," Brian spoke finally. "I understand it's all completely new to you, so if there is anything you want to know just go ahead and ask."

I had so many questions that I didn't really know where to begin.

"Do you spend the day in there?" I pointed with my chin towards the tombs.

He nodded. "Yes, it's necessary."

"What would happen if I went out into sunlight?" I continued.

"You would burn to ashes. And the same would happen if you caught on fire."

Wow! So when he saved me from the burning arena he was risking his life? For me?!

Next I asked about wooden sticks and silver bullets, and he explained that they wouldn't harm or kill us.

Brian was just in the middle of telling me about other vampire myths like crucifixes, holy water and garlic when the door opened and in came his companion. He was much shorter than Brian and looked quite unfashionable with his short brown hair parted and slicked back.

He gave me a hateful look and started to grumble, "Brian, for God's sake, why don't you ever listen to me?! We both know she will be nothing but trouble!"

I knew immediately which of the two was the nice one.

"Silvia, this is Alex. Alex, Silvia." Brian introduced us, ignoring Alex's outburst.

I nodded, not knowing what to say.

"How does it look out there?" Brian asked.

"It's good, they have it under control. Fortunately, the fire didn't spread," Alex replied and looked at me as if it was all my fault.

I wanted to say something to my defense but, realizing he had already formed his opinion of me, decided to let it be. Besides, I had no idea how the fire started anyway.

It was a miracle the flames didn't spread. Had it happened anywhere else, half of Mt. Diablo would have already been burning. Not at Theresa's place, though. Thanks to the horses and ponies tamping down the ground around the arena for years, a big bald spot was created which served as a perfect fire barrier.

"And Theresa's house?" I asked with hope in my voice.

"It's untouched," Alex replied.

Thank God! At least she didn't lose everything.

I had to find out if Alex knew something about Peace, so I asked if anyone had already looked for the horses.

Alex was surprisingly helpful. "The firemen caught two ponies and, on my way back, I saw a limping horse going down our driveway."

What if it was Peace? I thought with horror.

"Was it a big chestnut warmblood or a dark brown Thoroughbred?" I asked, not really believing he would know the difference.

"Don't know, I just noticed it was practically dragging its hind leg behind it."

"I have to call the owner!" I pleaded with Brian.

"I'll do it myself!" he said resolutely, spoiling another of my attempts to get out of there.

"Where is your cell phone?" he asked.

"I left it in my car," I said disappointedly. The last thing I wanted was to sit there and do nothing.

"Don't worry!" Brian tried to comfort me. "I'll find out if it's Peace or Mack and call Walter." As he was saying that, Alex threw him my Honda keys and he was gone.

I was totally confused. *Where did they get my car keys? And how come Brian knows all those things?*

"You know Peace? And Walter?" I asked Alex, who was starting one of the laptops.

"I'm not part of that," he replied. "It's Brian who's an expert on your life. He's been stalking you for several months."

"Why?!" I asked, bewildered.

"I guess he wanted this the whole time," he pointed at me. "To make you his vampire bride."

"I am nobody's vampire bride!" I protested resolutely, feeling highly offended.

Alex laughed viciously and began doing something on the computer.

Trying not to think about Brian, I sat chanting silently, *Not Peace, not Peace, not Peace...* I knew it meant wishing Mack to be hurt and I felt bad about it, but I just couldn't help myself. I wouldn't be able to bare it if something happened to Peace.

Ricky came to me and put his head on my lap, demanding my attention. I put my hand on his head and started to scratch him behind his ears. He seemed to like it.

Alex looked at us disapprovingly and muttered to himself, "You could've come to me for a scratch."

"Maybe he's afraid of you," I suggested, regretting it immediately. Something inside told me that being honest with Alex wasn't the best thing to do.

"Nonsense!" he grumbled and continued with whatever he was doing.

A while later he spoke again. "That accent of yours – where did you say you were from?"

"I'm from Romania," I said proudly. After all, it was nothing to be ashamed of.

"You are Romanian?!" he exclaimed as if he couldn't believe his ears.

"Yes, I am. Do you have a problem with that?" I asked, a bit irritated.

"Not really, but if it wasn't for that motherfucker Dracula, we wouldn't be sitting here now!"

"You mean Vlad Dracula? What has he to do with us?" I asked surprised to hear his name from a real vampire.

"We are all his descendants. He was the first vampire," he said, sounding serious.

"Oh, come on! You don't really believe that, do you?! Everyone knows he was no vampire!" I exclaimed, half laughing.

Although every year on Halloween, hundreds of tourists traveled to Transylvania to Dracula inspired costume parties and storytelling, in reality, there was absolutely no connection between Vlad III, Prince of Wallachia, and vampirism. We Romanians had never really understood why Bram Stoker made him a vampire in his novel.

"Of course, I know the story is fiction!" Alex burst out crossly. "But Stoker didn't choose Dracula for no reason. He was probably the only one who wasn't blind to all the proof that he really was a vampire."

"What proof?" I asked, not familiar with any.

"First, he was often seen at night near his castle after he was killed. Secondly, there is that document carrying Dracula's unmistakable signature dated many years after his death, and thirdly, his grave was found empty."

"No one really knows where he was buried in the first place," I argued, remembering a few things about Dracula from my history classes.

"Even if they did know, they wouldn't have found his body there," Alex insisted.

"Fine, so how did he become a vampire then?" I asked, still skeptical.

Even though Dracula was a tyrant and a sadistic monster, who had entire villages burned to the ground and thousands of his enemies killed in horrible ways (he didn't get the nickname "The Impaler" for nothing), that didn't automatically qualify him to become a vampire. If it did, then the whole world would have to be full of cruel vampire rulers.

"He was cursed," Alex replied.

"By who?"

"By a priest. Dracula sentenced him to death for a crime he didn't commit. The priest was a real saint, he even performed several miracles during his life. While he was dying on the stake, he cursed the prince to an eternal life in darkness and an insatiable thirst for blood. When Dracula was killed several months later, he didn't die but turned into a vampire."

"What happened with him?" I asked, starting to believe the story.

"He stayed in Romania for several decades and then traveled west across Europe until he ended up in Portugal. In the beginning of the 19th century, he sailed to America."

"Is he still here?" I was curious.

"No, he's not. In 1920, he burned in the sun in Alaska."

"A suicide?" I could understand that after more than four hundred years, he wanted to end it.

"No, one of his children."

"How do you know all this?"

"From my dear maker," Alex said ironically.

"Who was it?" I asked, eager to hear about other vampires.

"He was an old and powerful vampire. One of Dracula's children, too. But he made one little mistake – he changed me. He's not around anymore."

"Did you…?"

"Yes, I killed him," he said without emotion.

"Why?" I was quite shocked, but at the same time, I wanted to know why would a vampire kill another vampire.

The reason was much simpler than I would have expected. "He took my life from me, for Christ's sake! Isn't that enough?!"

"I guess it is," I had to admit.

"Did he change Brian, too?" I asked.

"No, I did – he was dying. But as it turned out, it was a really bad idea. Right after I changed him, he made a vampire from Ricky and now he brought you. My life would have been much easier without him!"

Wow, he saved Brian! Maybe he isn't so bad after all. He also didn't sound like he really meant what he had said about him. It even seemed to me that, in his own specific way, he liked Brian.

I looked down at Ricky, who was lying at my feet peacefully, and asked, "Are there many vampire dogs?"

"I doubt that. Changing an animal is strictly forbidden. If other vampires found out, they would kill us all."

Great! I thought. *We don't only have to hide our existence from humans, we have to hide from other vampires as well!* I didn't like that situation at all.

"How many vampires are out there?" I asked automatically.

"Not many. Blood sources are extremely limited these days," Alex replied and continued, "During the four decades I'm around, I've come across only five vampires. They mentioned another two on the east coast, but I doubt they'll be more than ten vampires in the whole US if I don't count us"

Ten vampires who would kill us if they knew about Ricky!

Alex went back to his work on the computer and even if I had more questions, I understood the conversation was over. I already had plenty to think about anyway.

10

The Decision

Brian returned with my things from the car and the worst possible news: "It's Peace!"

I sadly realized it was what I had unconsciously expected. Although I hoped and prayed that it wasn't him, somewhere deep inside, I knew that it couldn't have been that strong beast, Mack. He was practically indestructible.

My dear Peace was hurt, scared and alone – I couldn't waste a single minute. I started for the door but Brian was faster, and before I could reach for the handle, he was in my way.

"You can't go to him now," he said softly.

"I am going out and you won't stop me this time!" I shouted, determined to leave the cellar at any cost.

Brian looked into my eyes and put his hands on my shoulders. "Silvia, please, listen to me for a second," he said urgently.

I was suddenly paralyzed by his touch, my resolution melting in his blue gaze.

When Brian saw I wasn't going to put up a fight, he went on, "Walter's now on his way to pick up a horse trailer. He'll be here in half an hour, and then he'll take Peace and the ponies to some trail ride association. You know where it is, right?"

I nodded unwillingly. "It's the horse club on the Clayton side of the mountain."

"Fine, so there is no point for you to go out now and risk that some of the firemen will see you. I suggest we stay here for another hour and when things settle down a bit outside, we can go directly to that horse club and check how Peace is doing."

Despite being upset as I was, I had to admit it made sense. I hesitated a little but in the end, I agreed. "All right, one hour. Not a minute longer."

"Great!" Brian sounded relieved as if I had any chance to fight him and go outside without his consent.

"But don't expect he will recognize you," he warned me while leading me back to the sofa. "The Silvia Peace knew is gone. You are a predator now. Your smell, your look, everything about you will frighten him."

But I didn't care. All I needed was to make sure he was going to be all right.

It was the longest hour of my existence. Although Brian tried to entertain me by telling me how he had become a vampire, my mind kept drifting to Peace. *Is he in pain? How bad is his injury? Is Walter already with him?* Nevertheless, I pulled myself together a little and tried hard to pay attention to Brian's narration, as I really was interested in his story.

I just couldn't understand why Linda had cheated on him. He was a nice guy, good-looking, with a prosperous business and above all, it seemed to me that he had really loved her. *Relationships are simply too complicated,* I thought, always trying to find something positive about the fact that I'd never had one.

"But there was one good thing about losing my wife and my best friend before Alex changed me – I didn't have to explain my disappearance to anyone but my parents," Brian joked to lighten the atmosphere.

"What did you tell them?" I wanted to know, aware that I would have to deal with the same problem soon.

"Well, since I'd just gotten divorced, it wasn't too hard to make something up," Brian smiled sadly. "I called them, and told them I couldn't stay in my house full of memories any longer, so I've decided to sell it and do some traveling for some time. After that, I called them every year around Christmas to make sure they were all right. They also got several postcards from different places in South America – Alex's work. He is very resourceful. Would like a new identity? Want to multiply your wealth? Need to get something over the border? Alex knows exactly the right humans. He can arrange almost anything!"

Alex made a face. He took his eyes off the screen only when he heard his name.

Brian had mentioned that he was playing online poker. "Alex is one of the best poker players in the world. He taught me everything I know. We usually play at five tables at the same time." I was quite impressed.

"Are your parents still alive?" I asked out of curiosity.

"My mom is. She is seventy-five. But she doesn't talk to me. She is still mad at me for not coming to my father's funeral five years ago. Well, I don't blame her."

I wasn't going to be there either for my mom or dad when they would need me the most. But at least Brian had a younger brother. My parents had just lost their only daughter and there would be no one to take care of them when they grow old.

It was too painful to even think of, so I was grateful that Brian changed the topic and started telling me about how he had changed Ricky. It was quite a story! When he was describing how hard it was to teach him to control his thirst and how much time it took, I finally understood why changing animals was forbidden. A single hungry or poorly trained animal vampire on a killing spree would reveal our existence to humans.

Shortly before midnight, Alex closed his laptop and went to pick up a blood delivery. He won nearly a thousand dollars that night (an enormous amount of money for me back then), but instead of being happy about it, he complained that it could have been much more if Brian had helped him. In other words, it was my fault again.

He took Ricky with him and Brian left with them to check the situation outside. As soon as he returned, he finally let me walk out of that damn cellar. We walked up a flight of stone steps and entered the old cottage kitchen adjoining a shabby living room. Obviously, they didn't spend much time up there. I realized that in spite of the lights being off, I could see very well – I had acquired excellent night vision. Brian opened the front door and let me out. It felt great to breath in fresh air again even though it still smelled of smoke and burned wood. The only light outside came from the moon and stars, but I could see like it was the brightest day. I saw every blade of grass, every leaf, every little stone.

Brian started to run up the mountain and I followed him. God, we were fast! We made a big curve round Theresa's place, but at first, the view was blocked by the oak trees. We went further and then, suddenly, the scene of the fire appeared in front of us, and I stopped to take a better look. It was a sad sight. The only thing left of the arena was a pile of charred wood and the metal sheets from the roof. The tuck shed had burned down as well. The firemen were still there, putting out the last smoldering debris. My favorite place in the world was gone and with it all my dreams and plans.

I looked at Theresa's house that stood a bit apart from the burned site, gray and lonely, and felt even worse. *I promised Theresa to take care of her place and instead, I let her beautiful arena burn to the ground! What a way to repay her for everything she had done for me! What will she think of me when she returns and finds this?!*

"A lot of memories, huh?" Brian said softly next to me.

"I saw you on Peace, you were really good," he added.

"Alex said you were stalking me," I remarked accusingly.

"That's bullshit! I just liked to watch you ride..."

"Why? Do you like horses?" I asked, trying to make some sense of it.

"Well, yes, but that wasn't the main reason. When I saw how happy you were on that horse, it reminded me how great it sometimes felt to be a human."

"I'll miss it." I sighed, knowing I will never ride Peace again.

"I know," Brian said bitterly and we continued towards the Bells' house.

As we were approaching it from down the mountain, I noticed my red Honda was parked outside the garage. *Alex!* I thought. At the front door, Brian pulled my house keys from his jeans' pocket and we slipped in. He stayed in the hall while I went to my room to get changed.

I removed my burned clothes in the bathroom and checked my appearance in my movie star mirror. *God, I'm pale! And dirty!* At least my reflection was there – another vampire myth disproved. I cleaned up and put on my new jeans and my favorite blouse. I wanted to look nice.

"Wow, you look..." Brian said with surprise when I came back to the hall. It seemed to work.

Finally, we were on our way to the horse club! We ran over the mountain, and after several minutes came across the winding side road I had taken with Walter and Theresa on the 4th of July when we went to see the fireworks.

"We're getting close!" I informed Brian excitedly.

We followed the road down the mountain, and soon the Clubhouse and the pool appeared in front of us. We went around the back of the riding rings. On the opposite side, there were several open stalls, and in one of them I saw Spirit and Black Beauty. *Thank God! At least they are all right."*

The lights on the front stable were on and there were two cars parked in the parking lot. One of them was Walter's GMC with a two-horse trailer hooked to it. *He's still here!*

We hid behind an oak tree on the far side of the parking lot and listened to the voices coming from the trailer. I recognized Walter immediately and soon I understood that the second voice belonged to a vet. He was just examining Peace. *Why don't they take him out of the trailer?!* I didn't like the situation at all.

They were quiet for a while and then, the vet spoke again. "I am sorry, Walter, it's a comminuted fracture of the second phalanx. In addition to that, the flexor tendon is completely severed."

Oh, no! I didn't understand half of what the vet had said, but there was no doubt it was really bad.

"It seems he got his hoof stuck between two rocks up there, and did it himself while trying to pull it out," the vet continued.

"Will he walk again?" Walter asked with a strained voice.

"It's hard to say without an x-ray and MRI. They can fix the pieces of the bone with screws and plates and stitch the tendon back together, but the prognosis is still quite poor. It also depends on the extent of damage to the joints. They will tell you more in Oakdale."

I was devastated. It was even worse than I had imagined.

Brian, who was standing behind me, put his arm on my shoulder and whispered, "I am sorry."

I couldn't face him. I just kept staring at the trailer, frozen with pain.

After giving Peace some painkillers and fixating his injured leg for the transport, the vet came out of the trailer with a big medical box in his hand. Walter emerged behind him and followed him to his car.

"Thanks for coming in the middle of the night, Roy," he said gratefully.

"I'm sorry, I couldn't give you better news, Walter. Call me from Oakdale when you know something."

They shook hands, the vet climbed in his car and left.

I waited a moment to make sure he was gone and then shot forward with all my newly acquired strength and speed. Brian had no chance to stop me this time.

"Walter!" I shouted, hearing Brian swear behind me.

Walter, who was already getting into the trailer, turned around and stared at me with a surprised look on his face. I stopped on the edge of the illuminated area, immediately regretting leaving our hideaway. It was my first encounter with a human, and Walter turned into a mere sack of blood in front of me. The only thing I suddenly saw was the pulsing artery on his neck, all I could hear was his beating heart pumping blood through his body. I felt I was losing it.

But Walter's reaction was such that it brought me back again.

"Silvia, where the hell have you been???!!!" he started to yell at me while walking towards me slowly. "I tried to call you a hundred times!!!"

I had never seen him so angry. He finally found someone to blame, someone he could let all his pain, frustration and despair out on. "D'you have any idea what happened?!!!" he raged. "The arena burned down, Mack is gone and Peace –" his voice broke off.

I realized he was getting too close and started to move backwards while trying to find some words to my defense. But before I managed to say anything, Brian was standing in front of me, shouting at Walter, "Stop yelling at her as if it was all her fault! It was Silvia who saved your horses from the fire!"

"And you are who?!" Walter asked, taken aback.

"I'm the one who called you. I'm Silvia's boyfriend."

"Is this true, Silvia? You never mentioned anyone."

I stepped forward trying to act normal. "Walter, this is Brian. I met him this week in Clayton. I didn't say anything 'cause it was all too fresh, you know..." I lied.

While I spoke, Walter was eyeing me with a searching look.

"God, you look pale! What happened to you?!"

"I'm fine. I just had a little accident when I was letting the ponies out of the arena. Luckily Brian found me and helped me get out of there." I was surprised how easy it was to make up a credible story.

However, Walter wasn't done questioning yet.

"But where have you been till now?! The firemen said there was nobody home at the Bells' house!"

"She was a bit shaken, so I took her to my place to get some rest," said Brian coming to my rescue.

Walter looked around and, seeing no other car, he asked, "And how did you get here?"

"Silvia wasn't sure where the place was, so we left the car down the road," Brian explained.

Walter gave me a questioning look. He wasn't that stupid.

"Forget the car! I came here to find out what happened to Peace!" I said urgently.

Walter's expression changed. He didn't seem angry or suspicious anymore.

"He shattered the short bone right above his hoof to pieces and tore off the tendon that flexes the hoof. It's really bad," he stated gravely.

"But you are taking him to a horse clinic, right?! They will help him there!" Even though I had heard the vet, I still believed there was a chance Peace would walk again.

Walter saw it differently, though. "I am sorry, Silvia, we are most probably going to lose him. It's a complicated injury. The surgeries, the treatment and the hospitalization – we are talking about thousands of dollars here. I don't have that kind of money." As he spoke his features filled with pain and sorrow.

"Money's not an issue," Brian remarked and I looked at him gratefully.

"Walter, Brian has money. He'll help us. We can save him!" I insisted enthusiastically.

But Walter shook his head. "Silvia, it's not just about the money. I am going to do what's best for Peace. After the surgery, he would have to stand tied in crossties till the bone grew back together – he wouldn't be able to move for months! I don't want to put him through that. Not to become a cripple like me."

I had no argument to that. The last thing on Earth I wanted was for Peace to suffer. Walter once told me that he had a human soul and I believed it. He was so different from the other horses I had ridden before. If he became a lame horse, it would be the end of him.

I was at my wits' end – I couldn't bare Peace being miserable, but at the same time, I couldn't let Walter put him to sleep. Suddenly, I realized there was a third option. A crazy one as hell, but it existed.

"Walter, would you excuse us for a moment?" I said and beckoned to Brian to follow me.

We started towards the trees near our hideaway, leaving Walter standing in the middle of the parking lot with a puzzled look on his face.

As soon as we were far enough away and the nervous neighing of the horses died down, I told Brian what I had in mind. "We can change Peace like you did to Ricky!"

Brian's blue eyes widened in disbelief. "Silvia, that's not a good idea. Changing a dog is one thing but a horse?! It's a big animal. We have no idea what it'll do to him or how much blood he will need. It would be a huge risk."

Despite the fact, I simply couldn't let Peace die if there was the slightest chance he could recover.

"Please, Brian," I pleaded. "We must at least try it!"

"We have nowhere to hide him, anyway!"

"What happened to the cottage where you trained Ricky?" I asked, remembering him saying it was at some remote place.

"Alex still has it. It's empty now," Brian replied.

"That could work," he added thoughtfully. "But if Alex found out about it, he'd kill me for sure this time."

"Don't worry, he won't," I assured him, knowing he wasn't exaggerating.

Brian let out a resigned sigh. "Okay, we'll try it. But you must understand that if the situation gets out of hand, we will have to destroy him!"

I gave Brian a bright smile. I knew Peace wasn't saved yet, but at least there was still hope for him.

When we returned to the parking lot, Walter was in the trailer with Peace. I peeked inside and found my marvelous dressage horse standing pathetically on three legs. His right hind leg, covered in a splint up to his knee, was lifted up so that only his toe rested on the ground. It was a pitiful sight. Peace turned his head back and looked at me with his knowing eye. To my surprise, he was utterly calm and relaxed.

"Come on in," Walter called to me from the other side of Peace's neck.

"It'll be better if we talk outside," I said seriously.

Walter gave me an incredulous look. The Silvia he knew would never miss a chance to be with Peace, especially in such a situation.

And he was even more perplexed once he came out and heard my proposal. "Don't take Peace to Oakdale – give him to us. We can save him! We are his only chance!"

"Silvia, I thought you understood how things are. Even if you pay the best vets, they won't be able to heal Peace completely. And I don't want him to lead a miserable life."

"We have no intention of taking him to a horse clinic! We know another way to help him!"

"What way?! What are you talking about?!!!" Walter grumbled.

I opened my mouth, but knowing I couldn't reveal what we were, I couldn't think of anything to say.

"Do you want to save Peace or not?!" Brian spoke instead of me.

Walter looked me in the eyes and nodded slowly.

"Good. Then you'll have to trust us. The less you know, the better for you," Brian said firmly. Then he gave Walter the directions to Alex's cottage by the lake, and told him to meet us there at midnight.

"At midnight?! Why don't you help Peace now? Why should he suffer another day?!"

"I am sorry, Walter, but it's not possible. We have to prepare everything," I explained.

"Don't stay here, though," Brian insisted. "Everyone must think that you took Peace to the horse clinic and they put him down there."

Walter's eyes widened even more. He didn't understand anything anymore.

Before we parted, Brian gave him one last instruction. "If anyone asks, you don't know where Silvia is. Tell them that she called you yesterday and told you that she'd met someone and was leaving with him."

"And please take care of the Bells' goats," I added.

Walter nodded resignedly, and we started down the mountain.

"Silvia, you're not gonna say goodbye to Peace?" Walter shouted after me with a hint of reproof in his voice.

I turned around, and although there was nothing I wanted more than to go inside the trailer, hug Peace's long beautiful neck and tell him that everything was going to be all right, I said resolutely, "No, I'll see him tomorrow."

While we were slowly walking down the road pretending to be going to our non-existent car, I asked Brian worriedly "What if he's not there?"

"Don't worry, he'll be there. He loves Peace as much as you do, and deep inside he knows, we are his only chance."

I nodded. Brian was right. *He will be there!*

11

First Kiss

Once we made sure Walter wasn't following us, we turned up the mountain and picked up speed. We were in a rush. It was already two in the morning, and we still had plenty to do till sunrise.

Halfway back to our side of Mt. Diablo, we spotted something moving near North Peak. It was Mack, trotting down the mountain ridge, his head and tail held up high. He looked perfectly well and was evidently enjoying his newly acquired freedom. We could have chased him down to the horse club but, being concerned he might do something stupid and get hurt too, we decided to let him be and continued on our way.

We checked Theresa's place first. There was peace and quiet there now, with only two sleepy firemen guarding the place of the fire. We slipped into the Bells' house again and went straight to my room. I took out my old suitcase from under the bed and we started to pack my things. I bought so many new clothes in the States, that we could barely fit half of my stuff in it. I filled my travel bag with my favorite pieces and left most of my old clothes from Romania in the closet.

"I'll buy you new clothes," Brian assured me.

I smiled. My wardrobe was the last thing that worried me at that moment.

Brian carried my luggage to the hall and I sat down at the dining table to write a note for Amanda and Peter.

> Dear Bells,
>
> So much has happened since you left. I met someone and I have decided to leave with him. I'm sorry but I can't tell you where. Please don't look for me and forgive me for leaving so abruptly without saying goodbye. I truly didn't plan this.

As I was writing about my new-found happiness, I finally fully realized the gravity of my situation. I bent my head lower so that my hair covered my face and Brian couldn't see the pain reflected in it. I felt like I was about to commit suicide, writing this goodbye letter. The only difference was that I was already dead.

> Thank you for giving me a home,

I continued,

> and for everything you have done for me.
>
> Please kiss the boys for me.
>
> Love,
>
> Silvia

When I finished, Brian read through the note and nodded in approval. He took the house keys and my car keys out of his pocket, and put them on the sheet of paper.

"D'you still have my cellphone?" I asked, realizing I should leave it there, too.

Brian fished it out from his other pocket and gave it to me. "I turned it off. It's not safe to use it anymore. I'll get you a new, untraceable one."

"It's not mine, it's the Bells'," I explained.

I put it next to the keys and stroked the smooth surface of the table. *I will never dine with the Bells again,* I thought sadly.

Once we returned to the cottage, Ricky greeted us at the cellar door enthusiastically – they were already back. Alex was on the computer again, and when Brian told him that Peace was going to be all right, he just said, "Hmm," not paying much attention to us.

Brian turned to me and I nodded encouragingly.

"Alex," he started hesitantly, "Silvia and I have been thinking that we could – of course, if you won't mind – spend some time in the cottage by the lake."

Alex finally took his eyes off the computer screen and gave Brian an astonished look. "What?! I thought you were also looking forward to living in a city again!"

"Well, that's true, but with Silvia, things have changed a little. We'd like to have some privacy, you know..." Brian implied.

Alex eyed me with raised eyebrows and I just smiled innocently, feeling my pale cheeks turning red.

"And Ricky?" Alex asked.

"He'll stay with us, of course," Brian replied, taken aback by his question.

"Good!" Alex tried to sound relieved, but he didn't fool us.

"It's just temporary. We'll join you in a few months," Brian lied to comfort him.

"You can stay there as long as you want!" Alex grumbled and closed the laptop.

Brian spent the rest of the night on the computer ordering things we would need to adjust the lake cottage cellar for a horse. He told Alex that he was going to renovate it a little so that I would feel more comfortable there. He believed him since it perfectly fit his theory that women always cause trouble, and that nothing is good enough for them.

Alex was busy, too. He was on the phone organizing an extra blood delivery for next week. It was supposed to last the three of us a month, but with Peace, we had no idea. Luckily, the woods around Lake Sonoma were still full of deer and wild pigs, so we were counting on hunting.

Ricky and I were the only ones who had nothing to do. Ricky resumed to his place in the corner and I on the sofa. I made myself at home this time, realizing it was the only sanctuary I had for the moment. I didn't belong with the Bells anymore and I definitely couldn't return to my parents in Romania.

I was watching my new "family" while reflecting on the events of the past hours. *What a crazy night!* I was glad it was almost over. I wished it was midnight already, and I could finally do something for Peace. I just hoped that the painkillers would get him through the day. What was comforting though, was that he was with Walter. *No one would take better care of Peace than him. And soon, he will feel no more pain, and he will be my glorious Peace again! But what if not?! What if it doesn't work for horses? What if he becomes some kind of a monster we won't be able to control? What if we don't have enough blood to feed him? What if…* More and more catastrophic scenarios were popping up in my head and suddenly, I wasn't so sure anymore that it was such a good idea.

"Silvia, it'll be dawn soon," Brian said softly next to me, startling me. I was so lost in my thoughts that I didn't notice he had already closed his laptop and came to the sofa.

"Yes?" I replied, not sure where he was heading.

"You will have to share my tomb before we get you your own."

I looked at him wide-eyed, remembering what his closeness did to me.

"Can't I just stay here on the sofa?" I asked with hope in my voice.

Brian gave me an amused smile. "I am sorry, but we need to rest in absolute darkness to keep our strength. We sleep in coffins or tombs; burying ourselves in the ground would also do the trick. You can stay here on the sofa, but you'll be of no use tomorrow."

Since I needed to be strong for Peace and I wasn't going to spend the day in a grave, I had no choice.

"All right then," I agreed reluctantly and followed Brian to the "bedroom".

Alex was already "getting into bed", too. "Sleep tight," he grinned and pulled the heavy lid over him as if it was a sliding door.

I approached Brian's tomb. The inside was padded and covered in black silk. To my surprise, it looked quite cozy.

"Get in," Brian encouraged me while closing Ricky in his small tomb.

I lay down hesitantly to one side, making enough room for him. I had to admit it wasn't uncomfortable at all. Brian jumped in next to me and shut the lid. The tomb wasn't too spacious but we fit in nicely.

We were lying side by side like brother and sister, our shoulders, arms and hands barely touching. It was extremely romantic. I was lost. The only thing I could think of was how much I wanted to move my hand and touch him. But that would have meant making the first move, which I had never done before. So I lay still, hoping he would touch me, but the longer it took, the more disappointed I felt. I was already drifting off when Brian finally took my hand. I smiled and fell into a sleep deeper than a human coma, feeling sheer happiness.

When night fell again and I came to myself, Brian was still holding my hand in his. I was so relieved that it wasn't just a dream. I turned my head to him and his lips found mine in the darkness. I kissed him back and it was totally beyond my expectations. I had never done anything so exciting in my entire life. Before I knew it, we were kissing passionately while removing each other's clothes. If anyone had told me that I would be doing something so crazy with someone I had met only a night earlier, I would have told them that they had lost their mind. That wasn't like me at all. But at that moment, it felt absolutely right. All my principles, all my self-control was gone, and all that mattered was that he wanted me as much as I wanted him. That night I made love for the first time. It was absolutely fantastic and I wished it had lasted forever, but time was against us.

"We should get up," Brian whispered in my ear and slid to my side.

"No!" I protested, kissing him longingly.

He smiled and whispered, "I love you."

Coming from Brian's lips, the words got a whole new meaning. I was overwhelmed with emotions.

"I love you too," I breathed out and kissed him one more time.

Once Brian removed the lid and I started to get dressed unwillingly, I realized how thirsty I was. The magic of the moment was gone and we returned to reality. I remembered Peace and all the things we had to do by midnight and I was suddenly in a hurry. Alex was already packed and ready to set out for Seattle, and the look on his face told me he knew what took us so long. I had never felt so embarrassed.

After we fed, we loaded the tombs in the U-Haul truck that was parked in front of the cottage. They originally rented it to move to Seattle, but under the new circumstances, Alex let us keep all three tombs, taking with him only the travel coffins.

"At least I will have somewhere to stay when I come to visit," he claimed. For Peace's and our sake, I hoped it wouldn't be any time soon.

We set out shortly before ten. Alex went in the truck with Brian and I drove the pick-up. Ricky rode with me in the back, guarding the build-in freezer full of blood. In Clayton, we dropped Alex off at the garage where they had parked their van with the coffins, and he loaded his things and his share of blood in it. There our paths parted. Alex headed to his new home in Seattle, while we started for Lake Sonoma.

Brian went first in the truck and I followed him in the pick-up. From how fast he was driving, I knew we were running late. I hit the gas and prayed that we wouldn't meet a police patrol car.

When we arrived at the cottage at half past eleven, Walter's car with the trailer was parked in front of it. *Shit, he came early! Why can't he be late as always?!* We had nothing ready.

We closed Ricky inside the pick-up and went to meet Walter.

"How is he?" I asked instead of greeting him.

"Under the circumstances he is doing fine," Walter replied.

Thank God! I was so relieved to hear that.

"Take him out and tie him over there," Brian commanded.

But Walter had changed his mind. "I'm not leaving him here unless you tell me what you are going to do to him!" he said resolutely.

That was a complication we weren't expecting. Peace was still his horse, and even if it was for the best, I couldn't simply take him against his will. Not after all he had done for me.

I turned to Brian and said pleadingly, "We have to tell him the truth!"

"Can we trust him?" Brian asked gravely.

"Of course you can trust me! I would never do anything that could harm Silvia," Walter grumbled.

Ignoring him, Brian looked at me.

"I trust him. He is like a father to me," I said honestly.

"All right." Brian sighed and asked Walter to go inside with us.

They sat down at a table in the main room and I stood in the corner behind Brian, still having trouble controlling myself close to a human. When Walter heard that we intended to turn Peace into a vampire horse, he thought we were joking. I couldn't blame him, though, because if someone had told me something like that only two days ago, my reaction would have been exactly the same.

"Will you excuse me for a minute?" I interrupted his swearing and ran outside to the U-Haul.

A moment later, I was back with my burned clothes from the fire. I put it on the table before Walter and told him what had happened to me the previous night.

"You're telling me that he turned you into a vampire?!" Walter exclaimed with horror in his eyes. It seemed my demonstration had the desired effect and he finally started to take us seriously.

"Yes," I replied and showed him my fangs.

"Good Lord!" was all he managed to say.

He sat quietly for a while, speechless, but when he spoke again, he sounded utterly calm. "Thank you for saving Silvia from the fire, I guess," he said to Brian and then turned to me, "but I can't let you do the same thing to Peace."

"Walter, it's his only chance!" I cried out desperately.

"I know," he said sadly. "But even if ... It's just too risky, damn it! You have absolutely no idea what it will do to him!"

"It works the same for animals. I changed my dog and he's doing great," Brian argued, even though he had his doubts, too. It was a great feeling to have him on my side.

"A dog is one thing, but Peace is a horse for Christ's sake!"

Although that was exactly what worried us as well, we couldn't let it show.

"I know he will be fine!" I exclaimed, "Brian has access to blood – we will feed him."

"And where do you want to keep him?!" Walter asked skeptically and looked outside the window at the dense woods surrounding the cottage.

We discussed that with Brian the previous night and had a plan.

"We'll stay here just temporarily, till we find a better place. Tonight we'll make the necessary adjustments in the cellar, and we're also going to build a stall outside with a small paddock. That should do for a while," Brian replied.

It took a lot of time and many more arguments, but in the end, we managed to persuade Walter to leave Peace with us. I was so happy that I would have kissed him if I could. Instead, I asked him to keep Peace company a little longer and we got to work. To my surprise, all the material and tools Brian had ordered last night were neatly stocked behind the cottage. He explained that he had promised them a fortune for an express delivery.

We were moving at the highest speed. Although I did my best to help, I was mostly just passing planks and holding things here and there, and it was Brian who did almost all the work. He turned out to be a great builder. In less than two hours, he made an outside cellar entrance and a wooden box for Peace to spend the days in.

Once we were done, we told Walter to take Peace out of the trailer and retreated into the woods. Even from such a distance, it was a dreadful sight to watch Peace desperately hopping on three legs. Walter tied him to the pole and after saying goodbye, he climbed in his GMC. I suddenly wished he could stay.

"Ready?" Brian asked me as I watched the tail of the trailer vanish behind the trees.

I looked at Peace standing resignedly at the pole, and only nodded, suddenly too weak to even speak. I knew I would never really be ready to do something like that to my beloved horse, so there was no point in delaying it any further.

I pulled myself together and we sprang forward knocking poor Peace down to the ground. Then Brian pierced the skin on Peace's neck with his fangs and started to suck his blood. I was holding his head while looking in his big dark eye. He didn't fight. It looked as though he was reconciled with death.

Part II

2020

June 27

Fifty-three-year-old Diane Marshall was sitting at her massive antique desk going through the mail. She was fairly tall and slim, and as she gave most of her riding lessons on horseback, she was still in great shape. The office walls were decorated with horse paintings and training certificates, the shelves full of trophies reminding her of her riding achievements.

Diane was born in England. Thirty years ago she moved to the States to marry Jack Marshall, a successful businessman from Denver she had met at a party in London a year earlier. It was love at the first sight. They had a fairytale wedding and she became pregnant shortly after that. The marriage wasn't happy, though. Jack was away all the time and Diane raised their two kids practically alone. When she found out about his mistresses, it was the last straw and she finally found the strength to leave him. The boys were ten and eight years old then.

After the divorce, Diane decided to stay in Denver and return to what she really liked – riding. Being quite good at show jumping back in England, she wanted to continue where she had left off, but a lucky coincidence brought her to dressage and she soon realized it was the right discipline for her. Although both her sons took after their father and had no interest whatsoever in riding, she had their full support. She bought a good dressage horse and in a few months, she won her first dressage competition. Within three years, they reached Grand Prix level, and a couple of years later, she started with musical freestyle. Those were her happiest years.

In 2015, after placing in the top ten at US Dressage Finals six years in a row, Diane ended her active career to set up her own riding school in Littleton, ten miles south of Denver. It didn't take long and she became a recognized dressage trainer and a musical freestyle choreographer. She was also named a United States Dressage Federation (USDF) judge.

Dressage to music became Diane's passion. It wasn't just a sport discipline for her – it was a form of art. A form of art that deserved more than music from a CD. She was convinced that dressage performances would be even more beautiful and the spectators' experience even stronger if ridden to live music.

She flirted with the idea for several years until last year, when she finally decided to do something about it. She went to her friends from the USDF with a suggestion to organize a dressage competition to live music. They liked the idea a lot and as Diane was an honored member of the federation, the management put her in charge of the whole project. So Diane got to work, and the outcome was The Night of Dressage to Live Music, as she called it, which was to take place on Saturday, December 5 from 7 p.m. at the National Western Complex in Denver.

Although the prize money was not very big, and winners wouldn't qualify for the US Dressage Finals, it was considered a matter of prestige to be in the event, and twelve of the best dressage riders from all over the States had already confirmed their participation. Among them Diane's young talented student Nancy with her gray mare Mystery. Diane had been training them for over two years and hoped they wouldn't place worse than tenth.

Diane was going through the pile of bills and ads with little interest. She hadn't received any new registrations for the competition in several weeks, and since the deadline was coming close, she didn't expect any more entries. But then she came across a fat envelope sent from a P. O. Box in Sonora, Mexico. She opened it with curiosity and started reading a registration form.

Name of Horse: Dash for Peace and Freedom

The name rang a bell. Many years ago, there was a horse in dressage competitions with exactly the same name. She recalled the owner, too. He had suffered some kind of an injury after which he couldn't ride anymore. *What was his name?*

She skipped to the horse owner and read, *Walter Niederman.*

Right, Walter! That was him! But the horse must already be ..., she looked back at the registration form. *Born: 1999*

21 years?! That's gotta be the oldest horse in a dressage competition ever!

She continued reading. *Rider: Silvia Love*

Never heard of her.

Trainer: Walter Niederman

If she is Walter's student, she can't be too bad. What music did they pick?

She went to the list of tracks, and to her big surprise, she found only one piece of music: *Sergei Prokofiev, Romeo and Juliet, Act I, Scene 2: Dance of the Knights.*

Only one track?! That's suicide!

Music in musical freestyle always consists of several tracks. They are mixed together in order to fit the tempo of the horse's gates and performed movements. At high scoring programs, whole teams of professionals spend hours with a computer and video in order to compose the right music for the horse. Diane knew the Spanish Riding School of Vienna, where they ride to classical music, but that's classical dressage, which differs from the competitive one quite a lot nowadays. So she naturally doubted Silvia would be able to perform all the compulsory movements while keeping the tempo of only one track.

At least it's a classic! she thought, having the same view on dressage music like Walter.

As she didn't know the piece, she took the enclosed CD and inserted it into her computer drive. A powerful, foreboding melody filled the room. *Wow!* Diane turned the volume down a bit and began to check the application data in the system. All the USDF membership numbers were correct, and she found out that Silvia passed the Grand Prix level test on Peace only three months ago in California. Everything seemed to be in order and the enclosed check covered the registration fee. There was absolutely no reason why Diane couldn't add the thirteenth couple of contestants to the competition. In fact, she was rather curious about their performance.

December 2

Preparations for the first dressage to live music competition were in full swing. Organizing such an event turned out to be more demanding than Diane had expected, and she ended up sacrificing all her free time to it. But she didn't regret a single minute. She wanted it to be a dressage event to remember.

Luckily Diane wasn't alone in it. She got to pick her own people to help her with preparations, securing a smooth run of the night, and since she wanted someone she could count on, she chose her employees Jason and Kate. Jason was her assistant trainer and Kate worked as a groom in the stables.

In the morning, Diane summoned both of them to her office to give them an update about the Friday morning rehearsals and to discuss some details of the night's program. Kate arrived first and while they were waiting for Jason, Diane checked her mailbox. After deleting some junk mail, she opened an email posted last night. It said:

Dear Diane,

I am very sorry, but due to unsuspected circumstances, we won't be able to make it to the competition before 8:45 p.m. We would give anything to be there on time, but it's truly not possible.

Please excuse my insolence, but is there still a chance we will be allowed to perform on Friday? Perhaps if Silvia goes last?

Huge apology for causing you any kind of trouble.

Best regards,

Walter Niederman

"Damn it!" Diane swore.

"What happened?" Kate asked worriedly. It was her first job backstage and she was almost as concerned that something would go wrong as Diane was.

At that moment, the door opened and a young good-looking man in his late twenties entered the room.

"Walter Niederman, the trainer of Silvia Love, writes that they won't be able to arrive at the competition before quarter to nine in the evening," Diane announced to both of them.

"Well, they are out then!" Jason said confidently.

"Oh, no!" Kate exclaimed. "We can't lose one of the riders only three days before the competition!"

"What if they go at the end?" she suggested. "They will still have time to perform!"

"Not possible," Jason shook his head. "Every competing horse must go through a vet check and then there is the opening ceremony."

Diane knew he had a point, but she felt the same way as Kate. She didn't want to eliminate any of the contestants right before the show. Firstly, she had already announced thirteen couples and second, what would she say to the orchestra? *Thank you for rehearsing Dance of the Knights, but you won't be playing it in the end?* No, she had to do something about it! The rehearsal wasn't compulsory (it was just for the benefit of the riders) and she could excuse them from the opening ceremony, but the vet check was going to be a real problem.

She gave Kate a comforting smile and said, "Nothing's lost yet! After all, I'm the competition manager, right?"

"But...," Jason started with an incredulous look on his face.

"Let's get to work!" Diane interrupted him and passed them the list of horses that were arriving already on Thursday. She liked the boy, he was hard-working and enthusiastic, but sometimes he could be a real pain in the ass.

Half an hour later, when the meeting was over, Diane called the USDF. She got a red light for Silvia and Peace at first, but she didn't give up and kept persuading them until they gave her permission to let them undergo the vet check after their performance.

At 11 a.m., after a short phone call with the vet, she wrote to Walter:

Hi Walter,

I believe your reasons are serious, so I have arranged for Peace to be able to go through the vet check after the ride.

If Silvia is ready to perform by 9 p.m. at the latest, she stays in the competition.

Hope you won't let me down,

Diane

P. S. Send me Peace's negative Coggins test and a 30-day certificate of veterinary inspection.

Diane checked her mailbox for Walter's reply several times during the afternoon, but nothing came. At 4 p.m., she decided to call him and was quite irritated when he didn't answer the phone. An hour later, when she was already home, a new email popped up in her inbox.

Dear Diane,

I don't know how to thank you! You're amazing!

We will be there, I promise.

Yours,

Walter

Attached there were the two documents she had required.

Diane read the email before she went to bed and fell asleep feeling good about fighting for them.

12

Competition

"Nervous?" Brian asked Silvia, giving her a warm smile from behind the steering wheel. He noticed how awfully quiet she had been the whole evening.

"A little bit," she lied, trying to smile back, but all she managed was a weak grin. Actually, she was so nervous that, for the first time, she was glad she didn't have to drive. She wouldn't have been able to concentrate at all.

She checked the dashboard display again. It was 8:05 p.m. and the GPS said that they will be in Denver in twenty minutes. Their destination was uncomfortably near.

She was dressed in her best riding clothes, but she felt like a pig about to be slaughtered. She wasn't afraid of the performance, though. After all the years, she was connected with Peace so well that she didn't really need to use cues any more. She just thought about doing something, shifted her weight a bit and he knew exactly what she wanted him to do. It was one of the best feelings in the world, right after Brian's embrace, of course. What she was really terribly worried about was that something from their carefully prepared plan would go wrong, and she'd lose everything. And she had so much to lose! The last eleven years had been almost like a fairytale.

Peace's transformation turned out even better than they had hoped. He was quite anxious and restless at the beginning, but he never became the dangerous bloodthirsty beast they had feared he would become. The long walks in the woods they took him for with Brian had a positive, calming effect on him, and Peace gradually got used to his new surroundings, life at night, and Ricky. Once they discovered that pure blood was too strong for him, they started to give it to him diluted with water in a ratio 1:3. They reasoned that it was because he was a herbivore, and therefore his organism was accustomed to low energy food. He drank a bucket a night, which meant his blood consumption wouldn't be much bigger than Silvia's or Brian's.

Silvia began to ride Peace again about a month after he was changed. They found their way back to each other almost immediately and it was like before, but they rode wildly, tirelessly and incredibly fast. Dashing through the woods night after night, they soon scared away all game from the south of Lake Sonoma. Although she tried to avoid humans, they managed to spook a hunter or two before they stopped coming to those parts completely as there was nothing to hunt anyway.

Even Brian welcomed that Silvia was away for a part of the night, for he could return to playing poker and making money again. It was hard for him to concentrate on cards when she was around, and since Silvia had the same problem, every time he tried to teach her how to play, they ended up engaged in completely different activities...

After three months, they finally found what they were looking for – an old fifty-acre ranch in Southwest Montana. Built in a small valley surrounded by several mountain ranges, it stood hidden in the gentle slopes of their foothills so well that you wouldn't know it was there until you ran into it. It was the perfect place to peacefully live their "vampire" lives, witnessed only by the majestic mountains towering in the distance.

For Silvia, it was the most beautiful place on earth. The breathtaking scenery changed not only with the weather and the seasons, but also with the moonlight illuminating the mountain slopes, so riding there was always spectacular but never the same. It was hard to say if it was prettier in summer or in winter when snow fell and everything turned different shades of blue.

Not feeling cold anymore, Silvia started to like snow even more. Brian taught her how to snowboard and it became her second favorite sport after riding. While whizzing at high speed down the steep mountain slopes, they caused quite a few avalanches, so their consumption of boards was high. Once, they were buried so deep under the snow that Ricky had to dig them out. They had never seen him happier than when he found them.

But they would have never had their great home if it wasn't for Walter. He couldn't bear to lose Peace completely and visited them regularly, checking how he was doing. It wasn't easy at first, as it took several weeks for Silvia and Brian to stop thinking of him as prey, and even longer for Ricky, but it was very useful to have a human they could trust.

When Walter learned they had found a suitable place for Peace in Montana, he offered his help without hesitation. He bought the ranch for them and moved there with Mack. During the winter, he arranged all the necessary permits, and as soon as the snow melted, he hired workers to renovate the ranch buildings and to enlarge the small wine cellar under the main lodge. They also built a brand-new riding arena which was even bigger than the one at Theresa's.

The work finished in the middle of summer, and Silvia and Brian were finally able to move in. Silvia fell in love with the place immediately. The ranch was even more beautiful than in the pictures and the alpine meadows surrounding it were just blooming with wild flowers. Walter had moved Mack to the nearest horse ranch but stayed living with them as he started to train Silvia again. They picked up where they had left off and it was like the fire had never happened.

Unfortunately, Alex decided to pay them a visit soon and his finding out about Peace and his human trainer was inevitable. He was so mad that, for a moment, they thought he was really going to kill them all.

"How could you reveal our secret to a human?! You are a disgrace to all vampires!" he yelled at Silvia at the top of his lungs and then turned to Brian. "I can't believe I saved such an idiot! Why on Earth do you keep changing animals every time I let you out of my sight?!"

He cursed at them for some time and then went hunting. When he returned, he was much calmer, so Brian explained to him that they had everything under control. Mentioning how much blood Peace actually needed helped a lot.

All in all, he took it quite well. He stayed with them for a whole month and before he returned to Seattle, Walter and he had become the best of friends. Alex had always been full of surprises. From that time on, he kept coming once or twice a year for vacation. In fact, he was at the ranch now, taking care of Ricky and Mack.

At first, they weren't sure whether to tell Alex about the competition or not, but they needed his connections to falsify the data in the USDF database and Peace's health certificates. Although he didn't like the whole business at all, he didn't stop them either. Perhaps the fact that it was Walter's idea played its role, too.

Walter taught Silvia everything he knew about dressage in two years, and since then they had been working on choreographies to all kind of music. They tried pop, rock, even jazz, but it just confirmed Walter's conviction that, for dressage, classical music was the best. Their taste changed, though. Because the light, cheerful Vivaldi music suddenly sounded out of place in the middle of the night, they grew fond of darker and more dramatic pieces that better suited their vampire existence.

So Silvia's dream to become a dressage rider came true after all, with only one catch – she would never be in any dressage competition. But that was something Walter didn't want to come to terms with. He checked the USDF web pages regularly for upcoming dressage events, secretly hoping that one day, a competition Silvia would be able to participate in would appear.

And that spring, he finally found it – The Night of Dressage to Live Music in Denver organized by Diane Marshall. He remembered Diane from the time when he rode Peace in dressage competitions and was convinced that if there was a human who would let them perform, it would be her. She was one of the biggest dressage to music enthusiasts he had ever met, and more importantly, she never cared much about rules.

When Walter told Silvia about his intention to register them, she thought he had completely lost his mind.

"Are you nuts, Walter? You can't be serious! I mean, fine, it's at night, but how does that help us?! There will still be other horses there, not to mention thousands of humans, the vet… It's absolutely impossible!"

But Walter had a plan. She listened to it patiently and then said, "I'm sorry, Walter, but my answer is still no. It's simply too dangerous."

She had already decided, and Walter would have probably never talked her into it if he didn't have an ally.

"Silvia, you must go for it!" Brian insisted. "It's what you have always dreamed of!"

"Honey, I know you mean well, but I've already accepted the fact that I will never perform. It's no big deal. I am as happy as I can be. I have you, I have Peace, we have Walter and our beautiful home. I don't want to risk it all for some stupid dream," she said.

"It's not stupid and you know it," Brian protested. "I have never stopped blaming myself for taking your life away from you. Getting you in this competition is my only chance to make up for it. It won't be dangerous at all, I promise! We'll plan it to the last detail, and we will be prepared for all possible scenarios."

"But it will be cheating," she objected.

"What do you mean?" Walter asked.

"Peace isn't an ordinary horse. He can't be compared to mortal horses," Silvia explained.

Walter laughed. "They don't compare horses in dressage competitions. They judge against a common standard and since we ride differently, that in fact gives us some disadvantage."

"But Peace is so strong! We will get extra points for his beautiful movements."

"Well, that's true," Walter admitted, "but your conscience can be clean. You'll get no prize anyway."

"Why not?" she asked with surprise.

"You will be disqualified because Peace won't pass the vet check."

Right. The vet check! She had almost forgotten about it.

"I just thought humans should see what we can do," Walter added sadly.

"Me too, but it's not worth the risk," she kept pressing her point. "We will attract attention, what if someone follows us? What if other vampires find out where we live?"

"That's not gonna happen!" Brian assured her. "You just concentrate on your performance and we will take care of everything else." He gave her one of his sweetest smiles and she suddenly couldn't think of any other arguments.

The following night, Walter and Brian started planning, and Silvia had no choice but to get used to the fact that she was going to ride in a dressage competition. Nevertheless, she still secretly hoped that they would come across an unsurpassable obstacle and they would call the whole thing off.

Brian pulled over and Silvia knew they were just a few blocks from the National Western Complex. Afraid the organizers might still decide to put Peace through the vet check before the performance, they had to arrive there at the very last moment. Silvia leaned to Brian and they kissed.

They never lost time. They were still in love and happy just to be together, regardless of what they were doing. Silvia even started to watch baseball, and with Brian, it suddenly wasn't boring, also because they hardly ever watched the whole match. Brian shared Silvia's passions too. She taught him how to ride, and the rides they undertook together were the best, no matter how many times Brian fell off Mack.

The only thing Silvia regretted was that they couldn't have children. Even though her biological clock was still fast asleep when she became a vampire, she often thought how wonderful it would be to have kids with Brian. They would be a part of her and a part of Brian, and Silvia would adore them more than anything in this world. They never talked about it, but she knew that Brian felt the same.

They were husband and wife now. They got married four years ago in Vegas when they were hitting casinos there with Alex. It was Silvia's first face-to-face gambling and, although she had been practicing a lot with Brian and Walter, she was quite nervous. Luckily, everything went smoothly and they won a lot of money. Alex even said that Silvia hadn't been so bad for a girl, which she took as a big compliment.

On their last night there, Brian proposed to Silvia while they were making love in their Mirage suite. It was the most romantic thing she had ever experienced. Totally spontaneous, though, so Brian had nothing arranged.

They got their marriage license just before the Marriage Bureau closed, and within half an hour they found a free wedding chapel. To Silvia's great surprise, they had everything they needed, including a bouquet and rings. They borrowed a gown and a tuxedo, and then Silvia spent some time doing her hair and putting on some make-up. She wanted to look natural so that she could send some wedding pictures home.

It was the smallest wedding possible. Just Silvia, Brian, Alex as a witness, a photographer, and the registrar, who looked like Elvis Presley in his best years. They found it quite appropriate, for Elvis was already dead, too. The wedding ceremony was nice but rather short, and when it was over, Silvia and Brian became Mr. and Mrs. Love. You can guess who picked the family name.

The photographer took plenty of pictures, but because Alex was making faces on all of them, Silvia could send home only the few of just Brian and her. She was so sorry that her parents couldn't have been there with them that night, especially knowing how they must have felt about missing the wedding of their only child. They were great, though, and tried to sound happy for her.

They thought that Brian was from Mexico and that his visa had expired long ago like Silvia's. For that reason, they couldn't leave the States, otherwise they wouldn't be able to go back again. In fact, it came quite close to what Silvia's mom had feared would happen the whole time, with only one difference – her daughter would never come to visit them. It was really hard for her at the beginning, but lately it seemed she had come to terms with it. She even stopped talking about grandchildren, realizing she would never meet them anyway. Silvia's dad was more rational, although he often scolded her for having inferior jobs. He thought she babysat, walked dogs and took care of horses.

"With your education, you should be working in a bank, and not picking up dog poo!" he grumbled on the phone.

Sometimes, Silvia missed them a lot. It was so strange knowing she would never hug them again. She sent them money regularly, but that couldn't replace their daughter. Anyway, what mattered most was that they both believed her story and that they were doing well (for the time being).

Silvia hardly had time to savor Brian's closeness, when muffled bangs suddenly started coming from the trailer behind them.

"I should check on him," she whispered and released herself from Brian's embrace.

They jumped out of their SUV, and as Silvia opened the side door of the ordinary horse trailer, Peace greeted them with loud neighing. He was shuffling around nervously, looking glorious in his new saddle and bridle. No leg wraps, though – he didn't need them anymore.

"Shhhh...," she tried to sooth him, taking his perfectly groomed head in her hands.

"What's wrong with him?" Brian wondered. The last time he saw Peace like that was right after he changed him.

Silvia shrugged. "He's scared. It's been a while since he was around humans and horses."

"But he doesn't know where we are going!" Brian objected.

"He is smarter than you think. He knows very well that we are going to some kind of a competition," she explained.

"Will you be able to handle him?" Brian asked with concern.

Silvia gave him a reassuring smile. "You just make sure to get us out safely, and we'll take care of the rest." She couldn't imagine that she wouldn't be able to handle Peace. For her, Brian's arms and Peace's back were the two safest places in the world.

Brian hugged her from behind and whispered in her ear, "Consider it done."

Silvia stroked Peace's neck for a while and he seemed to calm down.

"We should get moving," Brian said suddenly, after checking his cell phone.

They got back in the car, and three minutes later, they were entering the gate of the parking lot behind the Event Center. That was it! There was no turning back!

They parked a little further from the other trailers, and before Silvia managed to take Peace out, one of the organizers was rushing towards them. He reached them just as they were leaving the trailer and spooked Peace. He went on a rampage but, having anticipated that, Silvia was holding the reins with all her strength. The human took several steps backwards, taken by surprise. He was young and handsome and smelled deliciously.

"Silvia Love and Dash for Peace and Freedom?" he read their names from a list with a shaky voice.

"That's us," Silvia confirmed and handed the reins to Brian so that she could get in the saddle.

The moment she landed on Peace's back, he stopped bucking as if by magic, but he was still quite nervous, so she got him into a trot and they started making circles around the frightened human.

"You're on in a few minutes," he began uncertainly. "Go inside through there and get ready!" He pointed toward the open entrance of the nearest building.

Silvia nodded and made her request with an apologetic smile. "Please, would you be so kind and ask everyone to clear the way for us? Peace is a bit anxious today, and I don't want anyone to get hurt."

The organizer gave Peace a disapproving look. "That's probably wise," he muttered.

Then he hurried back inside. Although he was already gone when he spoke with Diane through his headset, they could hear every word they exchanged.

Brian sneered and handed Silvia her brand-new riding jacket. "Go, baby! Prove him wrong!"

She put it on and looked Brian in his bright blue eyes.

"I will!" She was suddenly more determined than ever.

They made one more circle round the parking lot, and then she led Peace toward the paddock entrance. She shortened her double reins in order to get his full attention, and they slipped inside in a slow collected trot. Their path was clear. *Good!* she thought. The other horses were neighing nervously, but Peace ignored them, focusing only on the entrance to the arena ahead.

All of a sudden, a horse leaving the ring emerged in front of them. Both he and Peace stood up and started kicking at each other with their forelegs while neighing widely. Silvia got Peace to retreat, and after she managed to bring him down, they continued forward, making a big half circle round the terrified animal and equally frightened human. Once they got past them, the horse came back to the ground too, and his rider got control over him again.

At least he didn't fall! Silvia thought with relief, as they finally reached the end of the paddock. She stopped Peace a few strides from the arena entrance, and turned him so that he couldn't see the thousands of humans inside. As he was too agitated to stay still, she turned his energy into a piaffe.

While he was lifting his two diagonal legs way up above the ground in a regular rhythm, Silvia listened to the announcer introducing their performance and to the rider's anxious whispers behind them. Suddenly time stopped and every second seemed like an eternity. Finally, she heard their names and they could enter the arena.

Walter arrived at the National Western Complex Event Center among the first visitors. He hung out by the entrance until the very beginning of the competition, checking out the incomers, and before finding a seat in the back row, he made a round through the arena. He could relax now and enjoy the show. The place was clean – there were no vampires except for him.

He joined Alex's clan voluntarily eight years ago when his bad leg worsened considerably. The knee was killing him. He was constantly in pain and he could barely walk, even with a stick. It was becoming more and more difficult training

Silvia during the night, and then driving twenty-five miles each afternoon to Mack. But Mack needed him. He hated it at the other ranch, and as he was dangerous to people and other horses, Walter was the only one who could clean his box and let him out.

Surprisingly, it was Alex who offered Walter to become one of them. He proved to be a natural talent for poker, and Alex could always use one more player to increase his wealth, especially since he had enough blood for all of them, including Mac.

Changing Mack too was Walter's only condition. He couldn't just leave him to his fate. He brought him to the vampire ranch and they were changed at the same time – while Alex was changing Walter, Silvia and Brian took care of Mack. He became a great vampire horse. He was even stronger than Peace, and he loved hunting and riding into the mountains.

Walter enjoyed being a vampire as well. No more pain, no more limping and no more aging. But what was best of all, was that he could ride again. He regretted only one thing – that he would never make another dressage horse. He certainly wouldn't make one out of Mack who absolutely hated working in the arena. Teaching Peace was great fun, and he would have loved to keep searching for another horse like him, although he knew that Peace was one in a million. Especially that night, being at a dressage competition again (at the best he had ever seen), he truly envied Diane the endless training opportunities that lay before her.

Diane was stationed with Greg and Madison, her colleagues from the USDF, who would be awarding the prizes to the winners. Their table was located at the short end of the arena, next to the judges' table at letter C. In total, there were seven judges placed at different spots around the dressage ring so that they could see the horse from all angles in each movement (a common practice for top dressage competitions).

The atmosphere at the almost sold out Events Center was fantastic. More than seven thousand spectators were immensely enjoying the dressage to live music, and each performance was rewarded by thunderous applause. Diane should be satisfied! But she wasn't. She had a big problem – it was a quarter to nine and not a sign of Silvia and Peace.

"Have they arrived yet?" Diane asked in her headset for the third time during the break before the second last performance.

"Not yet," Jason replied the same as before.

"Damn it! If they aren't here in five minutes, I'll tell Rob to announce they have some sudden health problems," she grumbled mainly to herself.

The last present rider and horse entered the ring and started to ride to a nice orchestral version of movie melodies mixed to the horse's every foot fall. Diane tried to enjoy the performance, but she kept checking the time instead.

"They're here!" Jason finally announced to her two minutes later.

Diane let out a huge sigh, "Thank God!"

"Are they ready to perform?" she added quickly.

"Hope so, 'cause the horse is nuts! I doubt the girl will be able to handle him. They'll be glad if they finish their ride. Never mind getting a decent score."

"Really?!" Diane couldn't believe her ears. The Peace she remembered was one of the sweetest horses she had ever met.

Either way, she finally relaxed and relished the rest of the very nice ride. For the spectators, it was faultless, but she, like the judges, found several mistakes which would show in the final score.

After a short introduction, Rob announced the last couple of contestants, and Silvia on Peace rode into the arena in an exemplary collected trot. Excited applause filled the arena as they set out on their circle around the dressage ring.

Diane couldn't take her eyes of them. Silvia, who was seated on Peace in a flawless riding posture, was dressed in very unusual colors. Although her hat and boots were black, and her stock tie, glows and breeches white as required, she was wearing a bright red tail jacket that matched Peace's crimson saddle pad. It was totally against the dressage dress code rules, but it looked absolutely fabulous on the almost black horse.

It was Silvia's idea. She realized that since they were going to be disqualified anyway, she might as well wear the color she preferred the most and that fit nicely the dramatic music they had picked with Walter.

Dance of the Knights was the obvious choice. Not only was it one of the most beautiful pieces they had ever heard – not many composers could create a dark atmosphere like Sergei Prokofiev – but it also had a motoric rhythm that made it easy to ride to. Besides, the version they chose lasted only something over six minutes, which is the time limit for Grand Prix level musical freestyle.

The pair reached the short side of the arena, and Diane could finally take a closer look at them. Silvia was very young (must be several years younger than Nancy) and looked very pretty in her gentle make-up that brought some color to her pail vampire cheeks. Diane recognized Peace but couldn't believe how much he had changed since she last saw him. His coat was darker than she remembered it, and there was a fire in his eye that had never been there before. She admired the perfect proportions of his body, even though his rock-hard muscles were very tense. *What training have they put him through?* Diane wondered. *He looks much better than ten years ago!*

They finished their round and entered the ring, making a smooth transition into collected canter. Peace suddenly seemed much calmer and when they halted in the middle of the ring, he became utterly relaxed. While he was standing motionless, evenly balanced on all four legs, Silvia gracefully saluted the judges and then nodded to the musical director, giving him the signal that they were ready. The conductor got to work, and with the first pulsating beat produced by the brass instruments, Peace sprang into a brilliant Spanish walk.

Spanish walk?! Diane exchanged surprised looks with her colleagues. The Spanish walk is a classical dressage movement that is not defined for dressage competitions.

As the main dramatic string theme started to play, Peace continued marching while lifting his forelegs high and outstretching them in an exaggerated manner. It looked very majestic and underscored the foreboding atmosphere the music evoked.

The main theme started all over again, but this time, Peace performed the most beautiful half pass at walk Diane had ever seen. The lightness of the execution, the engagement of the hindquarters, the degree of the legs crossing – it was simply amazing. And what's more, it looked exactly as the best dressage performance should look like. Silvia just sat there doing nothing, while Peace was doing everything of his own accord.

That's not a horse. It's a ballet dancer! Diane thought as they came diagonally to the center of the left long wall and continued in half pass on the other hand. At the same time, she realized with regret that it was another movement that is not judged at the Grand Prix level. *What a shame!*

When they reached the opposite corner, the music started to escalate and the duo switched to an extended trot. The hall filled with excited applause, rewarding the beauty of the horse's powerful, but elegant movements. Yet Diane's experienced eye saw even more – she appreciated the great impulse and perfect symmetry of Peace's extended strides. With Silvia's light reins, the whole performance became a real art.

They crossed the ring diagonally in no time, and as soon as they came to the corner, the main theme returned for the third time, and they went into it in a half pass at trot. It was executed in such a way that it took Diane's breath away. She exchanged looks with her colleagues again, but this time, they only mirrored her pure admiration.

The main theme went into a soaring counter theme, and Silvia answered to it by leading Peace into impressive trot called passage. It always looks as if the horse is dancing, but only a few horses in the world could perform it with such lightness and high spring in the hind legs like Peace. With the music escalating, they made a transition into a piaffe and Peace continued lifting his legs way up above the ground in place.

The tension culminated. Silvia collected Peace more intently and got him ready. What came next was a supreme classical dressage movement never seen in a dressage competition. As the string instruments started going down the scale in a fast sequence, Peace stood up, then jumped up in the air and kicked back with his hind legs way up above the ground. The arena roared! Diane, her colleagues, the judges – everyone was overwhelmed with emotions. It was absolutely fantastic and totally unexpected. The only two beings in the arena that stayed utterly calm and composed were Silvia and Peace. They continued in their majestic Spanish walk in total synchrony with the music as if nothing had happened.

Before Diane could recover from the highest jump ever performed, a beautiful optimistic flute melody filled the arena. *The Dance of the Knights* entered into its second part, which was in stark contrast to the first one. In the ballet, it represents Juliet's entrance to the ball. Played in pianissimo, it was very serene and calm, and Peace followed it in a collected canter light as a feather. They made a twenty-meter circle at the entrance end, crossed the ring diagonally in a gorgeous cantering half pass and made another circle in front of Diane, who was absolutely charmed. But it wouldn't be Prokofiev if the foreboding main theme didn't sneak back in again. Peace performed a mighty canter to it with flying changes every second stride that nicely fit the metronomic rhythm.

The music escalated again, and the growing tension gave Silvia an opportunity to show the fantastic impulse of Peace's extended canter. While they flew forward like an arrow, they were rewarded by another burst of enthusiastic applause. It seemed the humans simply couldn't stop clapping.

The flutes began to play the gentle tune which illustrates Juliet's dance with Paris, but tonight it was Peace who was dancing. He turned around performing powerful canter strides with his front legs, perfectly matching the rhythmic string accompaniment that sounded like a beautiful harp, while the circle he was making with his hind legs was so small that it looked almost as if he was turning in place. It was the best canter pirouette ever done at a dressage competition.

They made four unbelievable full 360-degree turns, and when the melody paused in the middle, they stopped and started doing it on the other hand. The arena was in ecstasy, and stayed in it all the way through Peace's wonderful flying stride changes performed to a playful oboe solo. Then came another long sequence of gorgeous pirouettes and emotions went through the roof.

The Dance of the Knights came to its final part. As the dark leading melody returned, Silvia gently took the spectators back to the ground with Peace's amazing trotting half-pass. What followed was their unbeatable passage punctuated with the strong cadence of the music and Diane couldn't believe her eyes – Peace was lifting his legs even higher than before. With the last tones of the composition, they came to the center of the ring and once the final note was played, Peace halted facing the judges at letter C.

What a ride! Diane stood up among the first and started clapping excitedly. A few moments later, the whole arena was on its feet, including the judges and the symphonic orchestra.

A wide smile spread on Silvia's face as she petted her dancing knight on the neck and started bowing modestly to all sides. The deafening applause was far from an end when Silvia fixed her eyes on the end of the exit corridor. Brian was already there. Her moment of fame was over.

13

Escape

While the standing arena was roaring, the vet who was supposed to examine Peace joined Jason by the paddock exit. They exchanged admiring nods, and the vet put his case down on the ground so that he could applaud, too. Having watched Silvia's ride from his seat in the third row, he was absolutely mesmerized like everybody else.

Jason, realizing how much he had misjudged Silvia and her horse, was even prepared to pay her a big compliment when she came to them. But he didn't get the chance because the strangest thing happened.

Instead of turning around and going to the paddock, Peace started galloping in the opposite direction. He jumped over the railing defining the dressage ring, made his way through the gap between Diane's and the judges' tables, and a few moments later, vanished in the corridor to the main entrance. The applause died down abruptly and the arena became so quiet that one could hear a pin drop.

"Go after them!" Diane yelled in Jason's earphone.

Jason shot forward and ran across the arena towards the exit. When he finally got there, red-faced and totally out of breath, he found nothing but the wide open entrance door. He ran through it onto the street and, panting heavily, looked around for any sign of Silvia and Peace. Nothing! He jogged to the corner of the Event Center and looked up and down the street. No trace of them anywhere!

"They're gone!" Jason reported to Diane.

"Great!" she said.

The announcer introduced the Denver Orchestra musical performance that would give her colleagues time to evaluate the score sheets and determine the winners. It was one of the most famous baroque pieces from Johann Sebastian Bach called Air.

Walter listened to the enchanting music with a blissful look on his face. Everything had gone exactly as planned and the reaction of the audience even exceeded his expectations. When Silvia and Peace got a standing ovation at the end, he was so touched that he nearly broke into tears. It was a bigger reward for all the years of training work he had done, than any first-place award he could have received.

The award ceremony began, and all the competing riders and their horses entered the ring for the last time – all of them except for Silvia and Peace. Walter's expression darkened a bit. *They should be among them. They deserve it more than anybody else.* However, he knew all too well that they wouldn't get any prize even if they weren't disqualified. There were two mandatory movements missing in their ride – the collected and the extended walk (two movements that didn't fit the music) – and because of that their score would be quite low. But that was what they did. They rode to the music, not the other way around.

The winner became forty-eight-year-old Paul Stevens from San Diego with his horse Frederic 95. It wasn't a very big surprise since they were ranked the best dressage duo in the USA. Although their ride was great and almost faultless, they couldn't compare with Silvia and Peace, especially their canter pirouette, which wasn't half as good, and so the applause they received that night was noticeably weaker than they were used to. Nancy with Mystery came eighth, which was, considering the competition, a great success.

The first dressage competition to live music was over and masses of people started to make their way to the exits. Everyone was full of impressions and most of them couldn't stop thinking about Silvia and Peace, the phantoms from another world.

Walter, having no desire to squeeze with tasty humans, left his seat among the last stragglers. He had plenty of time anyway as he had to wait till the parking lot cleared out, so that he could pick up the trailer Silvia and Brian had left behind. Then he would join them at the empty warehouse an hour north of Denver where they had spent the day.

He was already heading to the side exit when he suddenly heard his name.

"Walter!" Diane cried out, dashing toward him across the ring.

She knew Walter would never miss his student's performance, especially such a special one, and so she started to look for him in the audience the moment Jason told her that he hadn't come with Silvia. When she finally spotted him climbing down the stairs in the middle of the long side of the auditorium, she recognized him immediately – tall, slim, wearing a baseball cap, his long grizzled hair tied back in a ponytail.

Walter would have rather fled but instead he turned around and exclaimed, "Diane!" His surprise was genuine, for this definitely wasn't a part of the plan.

"I think you owe me an explanation," Diane said all out of breath when she got to him.

"Diane, I'm so sorry for all the trouble we caused, but you must believe me that we didn't do it on purpose," Walter apologized. He really meant it, and he was planning to compensate her nicely, too. In a few days, her training center would receive a fat check from an anonymous donor, and although Diane would never find out who sent it, she would always suspect that Walter had something to do with it.

"Can you tell me why on earth Silvia couldn't stay for the vet check and the award ceremony?" Diane demanded, sounding somewhat angry.

Luckily, Walter had an explanation ready. "Because of Peace. A few weeks ago, he had a bad incident with another horse and since then, he hates to be around other horses. He gets so stressed that even Silvia has a problem handling him. We had an agreement that if she felt the situation was getting out of hand, she would leave immediately after their performance."

At first, Diane didn't believe a word he had said. In her life, she had met quite a few troubled horses, and it was never as bad as that. But then she remembered what Jason had told her about Peace's behavior in the parking lot and thought, *What if he is telling the truth?*

"All right, but you could've told me all that before the competition! We would've worked something out!"

"You are absolutely right, Diane! It was a big mistake," Walter tried to sound miserable. "Please, can you forgive us?"

Diane gave him a bright smile. "Are you kidding?! I came to thank you! Silvia's ride was absolutely amazing! Anyone would be proud to have her in their competition and so am I. It was the best dressage performance I have ever seen!"

"Thank you, Diane," Walter said, smiling widely now, too. "You don't know how much it means to us!"

"I'm just telling the truth! Next year you should qualify for the Dressage Finals – of course, if Peace gets better," Diane suggested. "As long as you show all the obligatory movements, you will definitely come first!"

Her eyes were shining with excitement but Walter smiled sadly. "Diane, Peace is an old boy, he will be twenty-two soon.

To be honest, I doubt we will put him in a competition again. He has shown everything he knows, and now it's time to let him enjoy his retirement."

"Well, it's up to you," Diane said, her enthusiasm gone. "But to me, Peace seemed to be in top form. It would be a huge shame to stop training him now." She looked Walter in his dark eyes and suddenly realized how pale he was. He looked good, though – really good. As if he hadn't aged a bit since she last saw him.

"How is your leg?" she asked, recalling his injury.

"It's much better than I could've hoped for, thank you," replied Walter.

Out of courtesy, he asked Diane about her life and she spent several minutes talking about her sons, the training center and her students. Then they said goodbye, wishing each other the best.

Walter was already leaving when Diane remembered something. "I assume that Silvia is not coming back for the trailer," she called after him. "Do you want to pick it up?"

Walter turned around and gave her a guilty smile. *I was going to do it later secretly but since you are asking…* "Yeah, that's probably a good idea. Coincidently, I happen to have the keys with me."

"I thought so," Diane smiled conspiratorially and called Kate to take Walter to the performers' parking lot where the public didn't have access.

Well, that didn't exactly go according to the plan! Walter thought, following his escort across the parking lot while trying to avoid frightened horses. He couldn't complain, though. The encounter with Diane was a very pleasant one, and the sooner he picked up the trailer, the faster he would be with Silvia and Peace.

Finally, they arrived at Brian's SUV with the trailer attached to it. Walter pressed the unlock button on the car remote control, but only the car's signal lights blinked. There was no clicking sound of the lock – the car was open. *Perhaps Brian forgot to lock it,* Walter came up with a logical explanation. However, as he went around the car to the driver's door, he smelled a strange vampire scent. It was weak and mixed with the smell of Peace, Silvia and Brian, but it was there. Something inside himself told him not to get in the car, but since the woman was still standing there, waiting for him to leave, he had no choice. He opened the door and slowly sat down in the driver's seat while scanning the back of the car. Nothing! He started the engine and left the parking lot with a bad feeling. He sensed another vampire's presence!

He hadn't driven three hundred meters when a small figure rose from behind the passenger seat. "Hello, my friend."

Walter stopped the car abruptly and turned back to face a funky looking vampire. He was wearing a long dark dirty coat and his messy, greasy hair was sticking out in all directions.

"Who are you?" he asked him.

"I was going to ask the same thing. I was expecting the boy and his girlfriend, and what do I find instead? An old vampire! Oh, forgive me my manners – they call me Lester."

Walter gave him a searching look. *How much does he know?!*

"I'm Walter. My friends have already left," he said dryly.

"What a sweet couple they are," Lester remarked with a grin.

"Yeah," Walter tried to smile. "You know, young love."

Lester shook his head, though. "I didn't mean the girl and the boy, I meant the girl and her vampire horse!" he clarified, stressing the last two words.

When Silvia and Brian arrived, Lester was just finishing a stray cat in the stock yards behind the Event Center, and the commotion Peace caused attracted his attention. He sniffed the cold December air and caught a mixture of human, horse and vampire scents. His curiosity peaked, he climbed on the roof of the once famous Denver Union Stock Yard Company building, from where he had a great view on the performers' parking lot. He hid behind the company sign and watched, soon recognizing vampires in Silvia and Brian. He found it strange that a vampire would ride a horse, so he gave the animal a closer look and couldn't believe his eyes – it was a vampire, too! He waited till they vanished inside and then creeped into their car to wait for them there.

Shit! He knows everything! Walter silently cursed. He was too shocked to react.

"Who is your maker?" Lester asked.

"Hakan," Walter uttered the name of the only vampire he knew that had no connection whatsoever with them.

"That bloody Indian?! I didn't know he changed anyone."

"He changed me a long time ago when he was in Mexico," Walter lied.

"Didn't he tell you that changing animals is strictly forbidden?!" Lester grumbled.

"Of course, he did."

"So I assume he also told you what the punishment is for this crime!"

"True death for the animal and its maker," Walter said matter-of-factly.

"Then you do understand that I have to report you to the other vampires!" Lester announced to him with unhidden pleasure.

Walter tried to stay as calm as possible. "Report what?! That you think you saw a vampire horse at a dressage competition?! They are already gone and you will never find them to prove it! You can either report us and look like a complete fool, or you can accept that we are of no threat at all, and gain something out of it."

"That you are of no threat?!" Lester exclaimed. "Not only did you change one of the biggest animals, but you went and showed it in front of thousands of humans! Have you all lost your minds?!"

"That was a one-time thing. It won't happen again," Walter assured him.

Lester gave Walter a pensive look. Although he didn't like Hakan, his motivation to bring true death upon three complete strangers and their vampire horse was rather small. He also had to admit they couldn't be totally incompetent if they managed to deceive so many humans.

If Walter had told the truth about Alex being his maker, the situation would be completely different. Lester knew the vampire who changed Alex well, and he was convinced that he had something to do with his disappearance. He couldn't prove it, though. Therefore, if he had found out that Alex was involved in changing animals, he would have a great excuse to summon other vampires and exterminate his entire family.

"So, what's in it for me if I keep it to myself?" Lester spoke finally.

"Money. We will pay you for your silence," Walter said.

Lester's eyes were suddenly shining with excitement. "How much?"

"Ten grand once a year."

Ten thousand dollars! That would solve Lester's financial problems! He would be able to buy a car, new clothes… Getting this amount every year would make his existence much easier. *But will it be enough?* He should ask for more!

"Fifteen grand and we have a deal!"

"Okay," Walter agreed.

They arranged to meet at the same place in two weeks and Lester left.

Walter pulled away towards the freeway while contemplating his conversation with Lester. *He can't be trusted. And he is greedy. He will want more and more. Anyhow, Alex will never approve such a waste of money. We have a big problem!* He drove onto Interstate 25, but instead of going north, he headed south. There was still plenty of time till dawn, and he wouldn't risk coming near Silvia and Brian until he was one-hundred percent sure that no one was following him. He had also decided not to tell them about Lester. At least not yet – it would ruin their night.

A couple of miles later, he picked up his cell phone and dialed a well-known number.

"Alex, we have a vampire to kill!"

EPILOGUE

Peace is standing calmly in the windowless back of a truck, chewing contently on hay. He has never minded traveling. His stall is separated by a solid wall and its entrance can be sealed by a heavy metal door so that it becomes an airtight box. The other section of the freight space is stacked with three travel coffins. Once the hay is totally chewed up, Peace spits it out again. He does the same with the long juicy grass at their ranch in Montana. It is very relaxing and it makes him feel like the horse he once was.

He spits out another mouthful and takes a long swig of the strange pink liquid they started to give him instead of water long time ago. It is actually very good and makes him really strong. Mack drinks it too, so it must be good for them. He is in high spirits. He did his best in the competition and it paid off – humans were clapping like crazy and his Silvia is happy as ever. And when she is happy, he is happy too.

After giving Peace an early lunch he more than deserved, Silvia jumped back in the driver's seat of their gorgeous custom-made horse truck. Once she set it in motion again, she finally felt the adrenaline slowly leaving her body. They were safe now – they had already driven more than thirty miles, and no one followed them.

Their escape was unexpectedly smooth. Since all the Event Center employees were watching Silvia's performance, Brian didn't even need to use the chloroform-soaked rags he had prepared. He just opened both wings of the entrance door, and as Peace ran through it, he jumped on his back behind Silvia. They dashed through empty stock yards, then across some deserted freight area and, in less than two minutes, came to their brand-new horse truck which Walter had left parked for them by the river. They loaded Peace and Brian threw Silvia the keys, knowing she was too agitated to just sit and do nothing.

"So, was it worth the risk?" Brian asked Silvia while smiling at her triumphantly from the passenger seat.

"Brian, it was absolutely fantastic! I still can't believe we had a standing ovation!" Silvia exclaimed excitedly.

"That doesn't surprise me at all! I doubt they've ever seen a better dressage performance. I missed the end, but I can tell you that the air above the ground was the best you have ever done! Walter must be so proud of you!"

"It's Peace, who has all the credit! He was great! He really put everything into it."

"You were both great!" Brian corrected her, petting her hand. "And we both know that Peace would never work so hard for anyone else."

"I know!" Silvia sighed, feeling bad about it. She was fully aware of Peace's devotion to her, knowing that he would do anything for her.

"He must be really sick of the arena. I should give him a break."

"That's not gonna be a problem since we're leaving anyway," Brian said, smiling.

"Where???" Silvia asked in surprise.

"To Vegas, to celebrate your success!" he announced to her excitedly. "I've already booked our honeymoon suite at the Mirage. We are leaving on Monday and Alex is coming with us."

Brian knew that gambling in Vegas wasn't the best kind of celebration for Silvia, but he desperately needed to be alone with her. In the last six months, she spent so much time with

Walter and Peace that he almost forgot how it felt to be her husband.

"Brian that's..., that's awesome!" Silvia exclaimed, trying to sound more excited than she really was.

Naturally, she was happy to be alone with Brian again, but the truth was that she had been looking forward to coming home and doing all the things they hadn't managed to do this winter because of the competition. Moreover, the downside of going to Vegas with Alex was that they would gamble all the nights, leaving hardly any time for romantic moments with Brian. And after all the stress Silvia had just gone through, cheating in casinos was the last thing she felt like doing. What she didn't know yet, was that Alex was suddenly going to change his plans, and she would spend two of the most romantic weeks of their existence with Brian.

"You'd rather stay with Peace, wouldn't you?" Brian asked sadly.

Damn it! Silvia silently swore. *Why can I never fool Brian, when fooling my parents is so easy?!* Sometimes she thought he could truly read her mind.

"No, it's not that!" she protested. Although she wasn't very happy about leaving Peace after what he had just done for her, she knew he would be in the best of hands.

"Peace will be fine with Walter. I just thought that we would finally have time to enjoy the snow. You know, that we would go snowboarding again, for long rides with Ricky..., I don't even remember the last time we had a proper snowball fight."

"Silvia, if you want to stay home, we'll stay home. It's your celebration," Brian said affectionately.

"No, I wanna go! We can do all that when we return," Silvia insisted.

She knew the trip would make him happy and that was what really mattered. Brian was the kindest and the most generous person she had ever met, and he deserved it more than anyone else. Besides, there was never a bad time to increase their family fortune. They had two horses and a dog to feed after all.

"OK, we'll go," Brian said with a radiant face.

And suddenly, Silvia realized she was absolutely happy, too. Not only did she achieve everything she had ever dreamed of, but along the way, she found much more – a great, loving husband and a place where she belonged. Of course, she would never stop worrying about what the future might bring – a wildfire, other vampires, humans discovering their hideaway, or that they run out of blood. But not that night. That night belonged to them.

Printed in the United States
By Bookmasters

Silvia comes to sunny California as an au pair seeking adventure and soon finds what she's looking for: one of the last places where the Wild West still exists. Here, she can ride the endless trails of Mount Diablo foothills with cowboys. Silvia always dreamt of becoming a professional dressage rider, and now, it looks like her dream might come true.

She never could have expected to come face to face with the supernatural in the form of a charming vampire. She wasn't expecting to find the horse of her life there, either, or the best dressage trainer she could have wished for. Everything might be falling into place—or not. Silvia will have to overcome many obstacles to reach her goal, but at what cost?

The Bond is a romantic, magical tale from the equestrian world, as well as a gripping fantasy. Above all, it is a story about the wonderful relationship between rider and horse, the importance of pursuing dreams, and the age-old human desire for perfection, no matter the price. Silvia has come to California for a reason, and surrounded by the magical and mystical, she might find her life's true purpose with the help of a horse.

U.S. $13.99

What went wrong with Britain?

An audit of Tory failure

Edited by Steven Kettell, Peter Kerr & Daniela Tepe

What went wrong with Britain?

Manchester University Press